COACH IN THE GAME

Ms Free TV

ISBN: 979-8-218-85887-2

Publisher: Ms Free TV

Printed in the United States of America

For more information, visit: msfreetv.com

DayDay
I did it!
You're with me always.

Daddy
If anyone asks who I am…
I am a reflection of your greatness.

Rest well KINGS

INTRODUCTION

They don't walk into my office to heal.

They walk in to survive.

You can feel it before a word is said. The curated confidence. The rehearsed ease. The designer armor. Women who run companies, households, and entire generations... but who quietly wonder, "Why do I keep choosing pain?"

This isn't about them.

This is about us.

Each conversation.

Each woman a mirror.

Each breakthrough a breadcrumb leading back to self.

You'll meet Camryn: the fixer who's grown tired of cleaning up other people's damage. Jenx: the rider whose loyalty nearly cost her identity. Navi: a beauty wrapped in luxury who fears she's unlovable without the packaging.

They don't know each other. But they all know the ache.

The silence.

The pattern.

And so do I.

These aren't just sessions.

They're exaggerated stories I've lived, loved, and finally outgrown. The names are changed, the scenarios stretched, but the truth is untouched.

If you've ever found yourself dimming to be digestible…

Shrinking to stay chosen…

Or pouring into someone with nothing left for yourself…

Then pull up a chair.

Because in my office, we don't do excuses.

We don't do confusion.

WE COACH THE GAME.

CAM | SESSION ONE
Dr. Hunter's Office | DUMBO, Brooklyn
Monday | 10:07 a.m.

Camryn McClain wasn't built for mediocrity. She was raised in the heart of Bed-Stuy. DeKalb between Nostrand & Marcy to be exact. Where corner store philosophies met concrete resilience. Marcy Pool on the corner of Marcy and Sugar Hill on the corner of Nostrand. The block was always a vibe, especially in the summer. She lived there until the big split.

Standing at five foot flat, she moved with the presence of someone twice her size. Honey-brown skin and hair kissed by the Brooklyn sun, curves like jazz, smooth, bold, and unforgettable.She had the kind of walk that made heads turn and silence prolonged. Not because she was flashy, but because her energy announced her before her mouth ever did. Cam didn't beg for attention. She wore confidence like red-bottoms, expensive, earned, and with a little arch.

But today… she was nervous. The hallway to Dr. Monroe Hunter's office stretched long. Her palms were sweating. She hadn't eaten. She hadn't blinked in what felt like ten minutes. Her heart was trying to outrun her composure.

The receptionist's voice was pleasant but robotic: "Camryn McClain?"

Cam nodded. "That's me."

The video screen buzzed. The soft female automated voice announced, "Dr. Hunter is ready for you."

Cam straightened her shoulders, took one deep breath, then another. *You got this, girl. Just don't tell her more than she needs to know.*

The door opened to a woman who looked like power dipped in elegance. Navy pinstripe suit. Nude YSL pumps. Jet black curls cascading down her back, with not a strand out of place. She smelled like luxury and clarity. Queening by Mind Games, to be exact. Cam instantly knew Dr. Monroe Hunter wasn't the one to play with.

"Ms. McClain…"

"Please. Call me Cam."

She sat down on the velvet chair across from the glass desk, legs crossed and purse perched.

"I was referred by a friend. She said… I was told you help people like me."

Monroe leaned forward, voice smooth as mahogany. "I don't help people. I coach the game. And Cam… everyone's playing, whether they know it or not."

Cam smirked, masking the tightness in her chest. She didn't come here to be seen, yet somehow, she already felt exposed.

The room was still. The candle on Monroe's desk flickered. Cam's reflection bounced off the marble tile.

Don't say too much, she told herself. But something in Monroe's tone, firm yet safe, made the walls start to tremble.

"Let's start here," Monroe said. "Tell me about the version of you that learned to survive."

Cam's breath was slow, measured. Not because she was relaxed, but because she needed a moment to line up her lies before the truth slipped out.

"The version of me that learned to survive?" She laughed, but it was thin. Fragile, even. "She was twelve. Woke up one day and her family wasn't a family anymore. Just a group of people living under the same roof. My parents split. My dad moved out. He stayed walking distance from our block so that he could see us daily. My mom stayed mad. And suddenly, I was… in between. In the way."

Monroe didn't interrupt. She let the silence do what it does best: make space for honesty.

Cam shifted in her seat. "We grew up in Bed-Stuy. After my parents split, we moved to Franklin Ave, across from LG (Lafayette Gardens Houses). Although right across the street, we didn't feel 'project adjacent,' you know? We had it all. The Lee jeans in every color, Jheri curls poppin', gold nameplates, and matching rings. Nike or nothing, that was the motto."

She smiled, for real this time. "My mom was the definition of strength. Ran the house like a sergeant and loved like a warrior. She was the disciplinarian, the chauffeur, the prayer warrior, and the HR department."

"And your father?" Monroe asked gently.

Cam's smile faltered.

"My dad? He was my hero. I used to think he hung the stars. Worked all day, handed my mom his check every week, and made sure we never went without. I remember counting his cash and helping my mom balance her checkbook like I was some kind of six-year-old CFO."

She paused. Something inside her shifted.

"But looking back… some of those late-night runs with him? The errands? The random stops at women's houses? I didn't understand what it meant then. I just thought… he had a lot of friends."

"Now I know." Cam's voice softened. "He was cheating. He'd been cheating. My mother knew, and I think… I think she broke in a way none of us could see."

Monroe's pen stayed still. No notes. Just presence.

Cam looked away for the first time. "She started making me tag along with my older sister everywhere. I thought it was just to keep me out of trouble. But deep down… I think she just couldn't deal with me. We were oil and water for most of my teen years. But it made my sister and me closer than close."

"And what about now?" Monroe asked. "Who is Cam today?"

Cam straightened her spine, like she'd been called on in class. "I'm a business improvement specialist. I help companies fix their blind spots. I own my own firm in Brooklyn Heights. I live alone. I travel. I mind my business."

"And love?"

Cam let out a breath that was almost a groan. "Whew, love. That's where the résumé gets a little raggedy."

Monroe tilted her head. "Tell me."

"I've been in relationships. Real ones. Long-term ones. But somehow, it always ends the same. I get cheated on. Ghosted. Or they "need time to figure themselves out" after I've already invested years."

Monroe nodded, slowly.

"And yet, you keep showing up for love."

Cam blinked.

"That's not weakness, Cam. That's resilience. But I want to know, are you showing up as the version of you who's healed… or the version who's still trying to be enough?"

The question hovered in the room like incense unseen, but unmistakable.

Cam didn't answer right away.

And Monroe didn't press.

Because sometimes the first step isn't the truth. It's admitting you're ready to look for it.

MONROE'S JOURNAL

Monday | 12:12 p.m.

CLIENT: Cam Session One

There's something magnetic about women like Camryn McClain. Polished, quick-witted, emotionally agile, but beneath the curated cool, I caught the flicker. The hesitation. The scar tissue dressed in success.

She leads with her résumé, always a telltale sign. When the heart's been mishandled, we pivot to performance. Cam is brilliant. Driven. But you can feel she's still negotiating her value in private. Still auditioning for the role of "enough."

What struck me most wasn't the story of betrayal. We've all been grazed by disloyalty in some form or another. It was how she told it that pricked my spirit. Soft enough to sound healed. Sharp enough to cut you if you listened too closely.

Cam's not here for validation. She's here because the pattern is starting to mock her, and that's where the shift happens.

Cam is the kind of woman who keeps receipts, not just in her handbag, but in her soul. She remembers the day her father stopped being perfect. The day her mother stopped being soft. And somewhere along the way, she decided that love was earned through effort, never through ease.

I didn't push her today. The silence did enough.

But I see the edge she's standing on. And I know that if she keeps walking with her eyes closed, she'll call it "bad luck" instead of an unhealed memory.

She's not broken. She's bruised with great posture. And next session... we're going to explore where she really learned to love conditionally.

— MH

CAM | OUTSIDE

Brooklyn Heights | 10:09 p.m.

Cam stood in front of her floor-to-ceiling windows, glass of wine in hand, wrapped in her favorite grey robe. The city glittered below, unaware. Unbothered.

But she wasn't.

Therapy had left a dent.

Monroe's voice replayed in her mind like a slow leak:

She wondered, *Am I auditioning to be chosen?*

She hated how that question lingered.

Like it already knew the answer.

Her phone vibrated against the counter.

UNKNOWN NUMBER

YOU STILL THINK IT WAS YOUR CHOICE?

Cam's chest constricted.

Her first thought wasn't fear; it was exposure.

Like someone had cracked open her private file.

She responded instinctively:

WHO IS THIS?

No answer.

She scrolled up to the last message from this number.

BEAUTIFUL PLACE. SHAME YOU LIVE ALONE.

She had deleted it.

It came back.

Her security camera app refused to load.

She tossed her phone on the couch and walked to the kitchen to steady herself.

A knock.

Three soft taps.

Not the buzzer.

Her apartment door.

She approached quietly and looked through the peephole.

No one.

Just a black box on the floor.

Wrapped with a red ribbon.

No name. No tag.

She bent slowly, heart pounding, and brought it inside.

Inside:

Red rose petals.

A flash drive.

And a note handwritten.

Watch this alone. You've already seen him. You just didn't know it.

JENX
Dr. Hunter's Office
Tuesday | 11:15 a.m.

Crystal Jenkins didn't choose the name Jenx; she inherited it.

Somewhere between her first heartbreak and her first coded drop-off, the streets started whispering it. Not because she was unlucky, but because her presence could kill.

Jenx grew up in Norgate, the six-story fortress on Gates and Nostrand: Bed-Stuy, concrete royalty. The laundry room always smelled like bodega bacon grease and incense. The lobby functioned as a therapy session, a dice game, and a runway depending on the hour. And from her third-floor window, Jenx could clock every siren, every secret, and every kid learning to dream beyond the block.

She knew what it meant to carry secrets that weren't hers, to smile at funerals she didn't plan, to count money that didn't smell like it came from banks.

Jenx didn't cry. Didn't panic. She didn't smoke. Didn't drink. Didn't flex for the 'Gram. But her man, Banks? He flexed enough for both of them.

Banks wasn't just in the streets; he streamlined them.

Quiet. Respected. Calculated.

Dangerous in the kind of way that made even old heads nod when he passed. And Jenx? She didn't just date the plug; she managed his back office. Payroll. Crypto accounts. Safe routes. She was the brains to his brand.

But even brilliance has a breaking point.

But Jenx, she noticed everything.

And now, she was noticing something about herself.

Something she didn't want to say out loud.

Session One

The receptionist clocked her the moment she walked in.

"Crystal Jenkins?"

"Appointment for six," she said, adjusting her Céline frames without making eye contact.

The buzzer was even softer, like a baby bumblebee flying near your ear on a warm spring day. The security glass slid open.

Jenx stepped in like she was entering a boardroom and a battle-ground at the same time. She paused. The scent hit her first clean, sharp, and warm. A Jo Malone's Nashi Blossom candle flickered on a sleek mir-rored tray beside an open journal.

And then she saw her. Dr. Monroe Hunter.

Monroe stood to greet her, wrapped in a double-breasted ivory tux-edo-style blazer with satin shawl lapels that kissed her curves like it was stitched in heaven. Her long black hair flowed down in soft barrel waves, polished like onyx, and her almond-shaped eyes met Jenx's with a calm that was somewhat disarming, like she didn't just read people, she de-coded them.

"You can call me Jenx," she said, standing instead of sitting.

"You can call me Monroe," the doctor replied, closing the distance with velvet grace. "But I'm more interested in what you call yourself when no one's listening."

Jenx blinked. Then finally, sat.

She didn't take off her shades.

Monroe didn't ask her to.

"Let's start here," Monroe said, voice smooth but surgical. "What made you book this appointment?"

"I didn't," Jenx replied. "My man did. Said I've been too quiet lately. That's his problem, not mine."

Monroe smiled just enough to unsettle.

"Funny. Silence usually isn't contagious unless it's covering something loud."

Jenx exhaled through her nose. That one landed.

But she recovered fast.

"I run numbers. Crypto. Logistics. I manage my life. I manage his life. I don't do breakdowns."

"I never said you did," Monroe said calmly. "But I'm curious. How long have you been the one holding everything?"

Jenx crossed her legs. Her heel tapped once, then stopped.

"You know who my man is?"

"No. Should I?"

Monroe tilted her head. Not playing dumb, playing neutral.

Jenx's smirk faded.

"Banks."

The name lingered like smoke.

Monroe didn't flinch.

But something flickered in her eyes just for a second. Recognition, maybe. Or memory.

"I see," she said simply. "And is Banks the reason you stopped sleeping at night?"

"I sleep fine."

Monroe leaned forward, elbows on her thighs. "Then why did you check your reflection in the elevator mirror three times, then put on shades?"

Jenx's mask cracked just enough to reveal a glimpse of the woman behind it.

She removed her shades. "You ever get tired of being the smart one in the room?"

Monroe didn't speak. Didn't move.

"The one who sees everything, plans everything, saves everyone, and still ends up apologizing for needing five minutes to breathe?" Jenx's voice softened.

"Yes. That's why I burned the cape."

The room was quiet.

Monroe let it linger. Then asked gently:

"What scares you more? Jenx losing Banks or losing the version of yourself you've built to keep him?"

Jenx stood.

But she didn't leave.

Instead, she walked over to the bookshelf and ran a manicured finger along the spine of a thick black volume. She stopped on a framed photo of Monroe standing beside a tall, dark-skinned man. His waves were sharp enough to slice through silence.

"You married?"

Monroe followed her gaze. "I am."

Jenx stared at the photo.

Then, almost too softly. "Funny. He looks familiar."

Monroe's spine straightened, but her face didn't twitch.

"I get that a lot."

Jenx nodded once and then finally turned around.

"I don't need saving, Monroe. I need silence. I need stillness. I need to know that if I walk away from him, the world won't swallow me whole."

Monroe stood up slowly, gracefully, unshaken.

"You're afraid of becoming your mother."

Jenx's eyes flashed.

"You never mentioned her," Monroe added gently. "But that's the only kind of fear that sits that deep. The kind that's inherited."

Jenx opened her mouth, inhaled slowly, then exhaled with the same rhythm. Then she closed it and let out a light sigh.

A low whisper came from her lips.

"She stayed with a man who broke her. Every day. In pieces too small to clean up."

"And you?" Monroe asked. "Are you washing, rinsing, or repeating?"

Jenx's lip trembled just for a breath. "Next session. I'll tell you."

She walked out with silence in her steps.

Monroe didn't sit.

She stared at the photo for a long time.

Because Banks wasn't the name that haunted her.

It was that flicker of recognition when Jenx said:

"Funny. He looks familiar."

MONROE'S JOURNAL

Tuesday | 12:21 p.m.

CLIENT | Jenx | Session One

Jenx is sharp. Not the kind of sharp that cuts. It's the precision that slices through noise, luring you with silence you can't avoid. Every word she gives me is lean, intentional, engineered for control. She doesn't waste syllables, and she doesn't waste time. She walks like a woman who has lived too much in "survival mode" and has forgotten what it feels like to simply live.

But here's the truth about control: it quivers at the edges. The tremble is always there if you listen closely enough.

When she spoke, I didn't hear panic; I heard fatigue. Fatigue disguised as discipline. A voice that's held too many secrets too neatly. She's been the one who "holds it down" for so long that her body, her mind, her soul, doesn't know what it means to let someone else carry even a corner of the weight. That kind of strength isn't fake; it's exhausting.

She mentioned Banks.

Casually. Too casually.

That wasn't a slip, that was a sigh. A confession wrapped in a name.

Her soul, unclenching just long enough to admit: I'm tired of being the only vault.

Still, Banks wasn't the earthquake in the room. The tremor came when she whispered:

"Waking up one day and realizing I'm just like my mother."

There it was, the wound that bleeds in silence. Not romance. Reflection.

Not fear of being unloved. Fear of becoming the template she swore she'd outgrow.

The mother wound is an inheritance few women volunteer for. It isn't just about what wasn't done; it's about what was modeled. Her mother baptized her in sacrifice and called it womanhood. Crowned exhaustion as intimacy. Painted survival as love. Jenx learned early that to be chosen meant to be emptied.

And now here she is, confusing depletion with devotion, mistaking stillness for safety. Her fortress is impressive. But even fortresses collapse from the inside.

The truth is: Jenx isn't afraid of men. She isn't even afraid of pain. She's afraid of mirrors. Because mirrors don't lie.

Next session, I won't dissect Banks. Banks is smoke.

The fire is elsewhere.

We'll talk about mirrors, mothers, and the cost of living in someone else's reflection.

Because therapy isn't just about finding answers.

Sometimes it's about handing someone back the questions they've avoided the longest.

And Jenx?

She's brilliant enough to see her own patterns, but tired enough to ignore them.

My role isn't to save her, it's to sit steady while she stops saving everyone else.

Truth doesn't shout.

It whispers.

It layers.

And if she listens closely enough, she might realize the most dangerous trap in her life isn't Banks, isn't men, isn't even her mother, it's the story she's still telling herself.

—MH

JENX | OUTSIDE

Bed-Stuy

Tuesday | 2:07 a.m.

Jenx didn't sleep much.

Never had.

Her mind was a maze that only ran at night: numbers, timelines, alibis. All moving in loops she didn't know how to shut off.

She lit a single candle on the windowsill. The rest of the brownstone stayed dark. Outside, the block was quiet. Too quiet for Gates & Bedford.

She leaned against the third-floor window and scanned the street.

Still parked.

Same SUV.

Matte black. No plates.

It had been there for three nights straight.

She zoomed in with her phone camera. The tint was too deep to make out a face, but she caught a glint of some movement inside.

Her breath caught.

She moved back from the glass, reached under her bed, and pulled out a fireproof box. She opened it. Inside was an old Sidekick phone, fully charged, along with two burner phones and a Glock 42. She hadn't touched any of it in over a year.

But tonight, her gut said, "It's time."

She slipped out through the back stairs, hoodie over her head, pepper spray in her bra. Walked two blocks to Madison before circling back. This was the only way to approach the SUV without being seen.

She crouched behind the corner bodega dumpster, heart thumping. A voice inside screamed, "Girl, this is crazy." But another voice said louder, "You ain't gonna get caught slippin'."

Then, movement.

The SUV door opened.

A man stepped out. Tall. Hoodie. Gloves.

He walked across the street and slipped a small envelope into a mailbox near the stoop next to hers. Not hers.

He never looked up. Never hesitated.

Then he got back in, pulled off without a sound.

Jenx rushed to the mailbox.

No address. No name. Just a single letter in gold:

"M"

She didn't open it.

She knew better.

This wasn't just about her.

And suddenly, she wasn't sure if she was the target…

or the witness.

PILLOW TALK
Knight & Monroe's Bedroom
Tuesday | 2:18 a.m.

The house was too quiet.

Monroe's journal still sat on the nightstand, half-open like it knew she wasn't done.

Then she heard the front door easing shut, deliberate.

Knight never rushed.

Even silence moved at his pace.

He came in carrying the weight of Brooklyn on his shoulders, every step a reminder that swagger isn't in the walk, it's in knowing.

"Why you still up, Halo?" His voice rolled low, gravel wrapped in velvet.

Monroe smirked in the dark. "Therapists don't sleep. We rehearse conversations with ghosts until dawn."

He chuckled, dropping his Timbs in the corner like exclamation points.

But instead of sliding into bed, he disappeared into the bathroom.

That was Knight; he never got in bed without washing the day off.

He didn't believe in carrying the street into the sheets.

The scent of his Creed Aventus shower gel crept into the room as he showered, bringing the smell of fresh woods, black currant, and quiet money.

She heard him humming under the spray, something low and untraceable, and for a moment she forgot every suspicion she'd written down.

This was the man she loved, disciplined, ritualistic, cleansing the weight before he gave himself to her.

When he came out, towel slung low around his waist, the scent wrapped the room. Clean, powerful, hers.

Knight kissed Monroe's forehead before sliding into bed, still warm from the shower.

His skin smelled like the version of him only she curated.

Untouchable to the rest of the world.

"You good?" he asked, arm falling heavy across my waist like a seal.

"Present," she whispered.

He smirked, Brooklyn in every syllable.

"That's therapist talk for I ain't telling you"

Monroe laughed despite herself.

"Maybe."

He kissed her temple, the taste of steam and Creed still clinging. "Maybe, huh? Don't worry. I know how to read between your maybes."

His heartbeat was steady under her cheek, like a metronome refusing to rush.

"Brooklyn was in my head tonight," Monroe murmured.

He didn't flinch. Knight never flinched.

He leaned back, folding his arms behind his head.

"Brooklyn always in your head, Halo.

That's why you fell in love with me."

"Is it still in yours?"

He turned, eyes deep-set and unblinking.

"Home don't stop being home.

Brooklyn raised me.

Brooklyn still breathin' in me.

Question is, can you handle loving a man who'll always belong to two places?"

It was scripture and street philosophy all at once.

Knight was always both.

Monroe pressed closer, whispering into the space between his heartbeats.

"Sometimes I wonder if love makes us sharper… or just blinder."

His lips brushed her hairline, slowly, deliberately.

"Both.

That's why it's dangerous.

That's why it's holy. Cuts you open, then heals you deeper than you thought you could be."

The room went quiet again, not empty, full.

Full of his scent, his warmth, his truth, and my doubt wrestling under the covers.

Monroe closed her eyes, letting his arms fold her into belief, even as her questions scribbled themselves in invisible ink:

The bed is clean, the love is real, but the secrets might be cleaner than both.

NAVI | SESSION ONE

Dr. Hunter's Office

Thursday | 8:28 a.m.

Time slowed when the door opened. She didn't walk in so much as arrive, like royalty stepping into a throne room that had been waiting.

It wasn't theatrics; it was rhythm, the way the air adjusted itself to her presence.

Navi Blu.

They call her "The Hood Princess." Brooklyn raised her; luxury crowned her. Most only saw the diamonds now, but pressure had shaped them.

Her hazel eyes, wide and luminous, Disney-princess shaped, were unforgettable. Lashes framed them like velvet curtains, drawing anyone who dared to look closer. They glittered with galaxies, but galaxies never revealed everything at once.

Her platinum blonde unit flowed in water-wave texture, silk in motion, each baby hair curving into quiet rebellion against perfection. Perfection was predictable. Navi was untouchable.

She carried a Judith Leiber Couture Albino Python top-handle, its clasp paved with diamonds. Rare enough as python, transformed by the diamonds into something more than an accessory, an inheritance disguised as a handbag. Bags were supposed to hold things. This one held legacy.

Some women tried too hard to be seen, and others hid from the spotlight. Navi Blu was something else entirely.

The kind of presence that rewrote categories altogether.

Monique Bluford was the name on her birth certificate. Born in Brooklyn, raised on Pulaski and Marcy. At PS 256, she turned hallways into runways before anyone had words for it. Even in hand-me-downs, she walked with a posture that bent the rules of what looked like couture.

Teachers called her "distracting." What they meant was she didn't fit inside their boxes. She wasn't meant to.

Everyone who crossed her path knew she'd live larger than the block. And she did. Luxury didn't stumble into her lap. She hunted it by any means necessary.

Now, seated in Dr. Monroe Hunter's office, she lowered the python bag as though placing art in a museum.

"Your office smells expensive," she said.

A Jo Malone Nashi Blossom candle flickered softly from the side table. Her tone, half compliment and half warning, made the sweetness feel like perfume laced with steel. Monroe asked if she liked it.

"It's delicate," Navi replied, eyes roaming Monroe's bookshelves like a jeweler inspecting cut and clarity. "Too delicate for me. I've always been more... oud."

The word hung heavy. Expensive. Regal. Fitting.

Monroe noted the flicker in her hazel eyes. "Scents that linger after you've left the room," she said.

"Exactly."

First sessions were always tests. For Navi, water was her element. She swam in it, parted it, controlled the current. But control was exhausting, and exhaustion eventually betrayed itself. Monroe's work was to wait until the tide pulled back.

"You've built quite an image," Monroe said. "One people can't stop watching."

Navi laughed, a sound melodic but edged with warning bells. "Images are everything. People don't respect what doesn't shine."

"Or," Monroe countered, "they hide behind the shine because they're afraid of the shadows."

The silence that followed wasn't empty. Silence carried weight. In it lived echoes of Kosciusko Street, the hum of her mother's voice, the rhythm of her block.

"I wasn't supposed to shine," Navi said finally. "Where I come from, girls like me disappear. Pregnant too young, broke, bitter. I wasn't doing that."

"So you became Navi Blu."

She tilted her head, lips curving into a knowing smile. "The Hood Princess."

It wasn't arrogance. It was armor.

Monroe studied her. "Princesses inherit crowns. Queens earn them. Which means you're still in transition. The question is, from what and into what?"

Her eyes narrowed. Challenge was not something she often met.

"Monroe," she said, voice low but steady. "Do you know what it's like to be watched your whole life? Every hallway, every bodega, every project window, eyes waiting to see if you'll fold? I couldn't just survive. I had to excel. Otherwise, they'd eat me alive."

"And now?"

She crossed her legs, the diamond clasp catching light like a third presence in the room.

"Now they watch from behind screens. The hood watches. Paris, Milan, Dubai watches. I've been visible too long to disappear."

"Which means," Monroe said, leaning slightly forward, "you've also been hiding for just as long."

The words struck.

Navi blinked slowly, deliberating like someone weighing whether to unsheathe a blade.

"You think I'm hiding?"

"I think the Hood Princess is a crown. But crowns are heavy. My question is, who carries Monique?"

A shimmer cracked in her untouchable glow. Not gone, but fractured enough to glimpse the woman beneath.

"Nobody," she said, her breath steady but sharp. "That's the point."

The paradox of Navi Blu revealed itself: the Hood Princess raised on Kosciusko, crowned in diamonds, carrying bags worth more than homes, yet uncertain whether her own heart was worth the same effort.

When the session ended, she adjusted her platinum waves in the mirror and rose as though stepping onto another runway.

Untouchable. Regal.

"Same time next week?" Monroe asked.

"We'll see, Doc. Royalty doesn't keep calendars."

She left, but the python bag wasn't what lingered.

It was the image of the little girl from PS 256, walking hallways with too much light for the block around her.

A light that people couldn't stop staring at.

A light still waiting to be held.

MONROE'S JOURNAL

Thursday | 11:04 a.m.

CLIENT | Navi | Session One

Some days, I wonder if I'm taking notes on my clients or if my clients are taking notes on me. Therapy is supposed to be a mirror, but lately, I feel like the glass is two-way. I'm looking at them, and somehow they're reflecting me.

Navi Blu sat in my chair today, dripping diamonds, carrying a python bag, and talking like she was untouchable. But I saw the fracture before she did. I always do. That's the curse of being good at this. I can smell cracks like rain.

And here's the irony: the same wisdom I serve them in neat soundbites is the wisdom I refuse to taste myself.

- Strong doesn't mean silent; it means speaking without begging.
- Luxury can hide wounds, but it can't heal them.
- The crown you wear in public shouldn't strangle you in private.

I give these lines away like communion wafers, but when I need them, I pretend I'm fasting.

Therapists don't get Spidey senses. We get knots in the stomach. And mine hasn't stopped pulling since I smelled Oud for Greatness on Navi's wrists, the same cologne that lingers on Knight's jackets. Coincidence is a lazy liar. My intuition is too educated to call it chance.

And yet, I love him. God help me, I love him with the kind of love that feels predestined, stitched into my veins. Love that makes silence feel safer than questions.

I write this because it's more secure on paper than in his face. Because journals don't flinch. Because if I asked Knight outright, he'd look at me with those deep eyes and say something smooth enough to rock me back to sleep. And I'd let him. That's the part that terrifies me most: I trust him enough to doubt myself.

The good book says, "The truth will make you free." But I've learned the half-truth keeps you comfortable. And comfort is the most seductive drug I know.

So tonight I'm writing down what I can't pray out loud:

"Lord, give me the courage to believe what I see and the wisdom to question what I want. Because love blinds faster than lust, and silence cuts deeper than lies."

I tell my clients all the time, "We don't heal by avoiding the wound. We heal by cleaning it out."

But here I am, staring at my own infection, dressing it up in designer sheets, and calling it devotion.

Tomorrow, I'll put my heels on, light my Jo Malone candle, and preach self-worth like scripture. But tonight, it's just me, my pen, my God, and the quiet suspicion that my heart might be the patient I've been avoiding.

— MH

NAVI | OUTSIDE

Madison Avenue, East Side

Thursday | 6:47 p.m.

The city was chaos. Horns blaring, steam hissing from grates, taxis slicing lanes like survival was a sport. But Navi's world? It moved like a private screening. Silent. Curated. Every frame adjusted until reality obeyed her mood board.

She stepped out of the matte black SUV, oxblood red Louboutin booties striking the pavement like gavel knocks. The sound wasn't footsteps. It was a verdict.

The doorman at 890 Madison didn't just open the door; he executed a ritual. Shoulders squared, eyes low, posture reverent. Not because he knew her name. Navi didn't pay for fame; she paid for invisibility that still demanded awe.

The elevator hummed upward, walls of gold-trimmed mirrors reflecting her image back at her. Platinum water-wave unit tumbling like liquid silk, baby hair rebelliously curling at the edges like commas in a story she refused to end. Hazel eyes wide, innocent if you weren't smart enough to notice they were armored with history. Disney princess eyes, yes. But this princess didn't wait for rescue. She built her own castle and charged admission at the door.

Her penthouse sighed open with the hush of hydraulics. A place too polished to feel lived in. Marble floors that swallowed sound. Smoke-glass bar carts stocked like confessionals. Fresh orchids. White, delicate, recurring, delivered every Friday, because beauty had to be scheduled.

She placed the Judith Leiber Couture python on its pedestal. Not a bag. An artifact. A silent sermon that preached: I won by outlasting you.

The air was thick with Byredo's Casablanca Lily layered over the echo of Oud for Greatness.

In the past, Knight never stayed the night. He didn't have to. His cologne lingered like a ghost with better boundaries.

Navi poured herself a Château Pétrus in Riedel crystal. Red so deep it looked like it had crawled through centuries to reach her lips. She wasn't drinking to relax. She was drinking to stay upright in her own museum of perfection.

The phone buzzed.

Unknown number.

One ping.

A location.

Clinton Hill.

Her face didn't flinch. She'd trained her features like soldiers. Queens never fold. Panic was for peasants.

But her stomach coiled, memory unspooling before she could stop it.

FLASHBACK

PS 256 | Kosciusko and Nostrand

Sneakers squeaking down scuffed hallways, beads clacking in her hair like warning bells. Back then, she was Monique Bluford, the girl who never blended, even when she wanted to. Teachers called her "too much." Kids called her "extra." She called it destiny.

They named her the Hood Princess before she could spell "royalty." Her crown wasn't Cartier back then, it was corner-store candy rings, double-dutch ropes cutting air like applause, and the kind of defiance you can't teach, only inherit.

And even then, always, always, eyes followed her. Boys leaned on lockers, pretending they weren't staring. Girls studied her like competition. But there was one older, quieter, who never looked at her like prey. His gaze wasn't hungry; it was calculating, patient, watching her like she was a storm rolling in. Dangerous. Beautiful. Unstoppable.

She never asked his name. Didn't need to. Some presences don't introduce themselves; they hover like a warning or a prophecy.

Even as a child, she understood the Malcolm X sermon without ever reading it: by any means necessary. Her walk said it before her words did. Her very survival preached it. And survival, she learned early, could look a lot like seduction.

The memory dissolved, swallowed by the skyline outside her penthouse window.

Vinyl crackled behind her. Micki Miller's "All I Need." Not digital. Navi didn't stream her pain. She demanded it raw, scratches included.

She slipped the Cartier Juste un Clou off her finger. A nail twisted into jewelry. Luxury pretending not to be bondage. She used to flaunt it, claiming she'd bought it herself. Independence as performance art. But the truth? It was a gift from a man who disappeared faster than his promises.

Her steps carried her to the walk-in closet. The part no stylist ever saw. The drawer no assistant dared open.

Inside:

- A burner phone.
- A passport with a different last name.
- A folded slip of paper with five words in unfamiliar handwriting:

If she ever finds out.

The words pulsed. She held them like they were hot metal. Still, her face didn't break.

Navi never cried in front of beauty. And her life, every polished inch of it, was a gallery of curated lies.

But cracks don't ask permission. They arrive.

Not a scream. Not a sob. Just a whisper, almost lost against the orchids, the marble, the skyline.

"Am I the problem… or the prophecy?"

Her voice trembled once, then steadied. She drew in a breath, and out came the mantra she never shared out loud, the one that stitched her contradictions together.

"God didn't crown me so I could break. He crowned me so I could bend and snap back prettier. Diamonds don't pray for pressure, they thank Him for it."

It was half-faith, half-sarcasm, but entirely her survival.

The orchids held their silence. The wine burned without comfort. The city glittered, deaf and indifferent.

And somewhere back in Clinton Hill, in the same streets where little Monique first walked like she had diamonds in her veins, the silence waited. Heavy. Knowing. Ready to be broken.

BREADCRUMB

Monroe's Home | DUMBO, Brooklyn

Friday | 9:19 p.m.

The wind knocked twice before the door ever did.

Monroe paused mid-sentence in her journal. Her pen hovered. The soft hum of CoCo Jones playing from the kitchen speaker suddenly cut off. No glitch. Just silence, like the house was holding its breath.

Knight was in the shower upstairs. Water running. No footsteps.

Then came the actual knock.

Three sharp taps.

She stood.

The hallway light flickered as she approached the front door, barefoot, heartbeat growing louder than her steps. She looked through the peephole.

No one.

But something was there.

A black envelope, thick, matte, and ominous, centered on the welcome mat like it had been placed, not dropped.

No markings.

No address.

No handwriting.

No smudges from a delivery glove.

She unlocked the door and stepped into the hall. It was empty.

No retreating elevator hum. No stairwell clicks. Just the lingering scent of someone expensive.

Oud. Sharp. Familiar.

She picked up the envelope and closed the door behind her.

Inside was a single card, jet black. Silver ink.

No return name. No salutation.

Just six words.

They've already been in the room.

CAM | SESSION TWO

Dr. Hunter's Office

Monday | 5:05 p.m.

Cam entered the room like she owned it, but dropped into the velvet chair like she didn't belong anywhere.

Black Nike tech fit. Gold bamboo earrings with "Cam" hollowed in script. Ginger colored side-part bob with a honey skunk stripe. No makeup, just raw Brooklyn skin and brown eyes that carried something higher than sleep.

She exhaled hard. "Yo, I don't even know why I came back…"

Monroe didn't flinch. Her tone was water, calm, steady, but deep enough to drown in.

"But you're here. So let's figure it out together."

Cam's jaw tightened, but her shoulders softened. She let the silence stretch like a test. Then…

"You ever feel like men fall in love with your potential but stay for the perks?"

Monroe let the air thicken. No rush. Silence had its own weight.

Cam muttered under her breath. "Like… I know I'm that chick. Loyal. Fine. Brilliant. But after a while, I started asking myself, did they love me, or did they just love that I knew how to make everything feel like home?"

Monroe tilted her head. "What does home feel like to you, Cam?"

Cam's lips trembled before her voice did.

"Safe. Warm. Smelling like Sunday soul food and purple Fabuloso. Home was my daddy ironing my uniform before school, sliding my lunch card into my book bag so I wouldn't forget. Home was knowing somebody cared enough to think for me."

Monroe's eyes narrowed slightly.

"Did anyone in your adult life ever make you feel that way again?"

Cam's throat tightened. She nodded, slowly, carefully.

"Once. A long time ago. He wasn't mine, though. He belonged to the streets. Never said much, but I felt safe around him. Like nobody could touch me."

Her laugh was sharp, empty.

"Whole world could've been burning, but if he was standing next to me, I'd believe we were good."

Monroe leaned back, face composed, though her fingers gripped the pen tighter.

"What was his name?"

Cam's eyes glazed with memory.

"He never used his real name. Went by some nickname. Sounded more like a warning than a word. Only knew him for one summer. My cousin's car broke down, and he fixed it like it was nothing. After that, he'd just… show up. Not trying to bag me, not asking for anything. Just looking out."

She smirked at the floor.

"One night, I'm heading to Lindenwood Diner. Some clown tried to press me. Dude stepped in and told him I was spoken for. I wasn't. But I ain't never corrected him."

Monroe's pen pressed into paper, carving one word: Knight.

Cam's voice dipped lower.

"He was tall. Chocolate. Wore black Timbs even in July. Always smelled like money but drove some busted car like it was a disguise. Mysterious. I used to call him Brooklyn Batman. He'd be there, then gone. No explanation."

Her laugh broke.

"And just like that, after Labor Day, he disappeared. No goodbye. No reason. Just vanished back into the city like he was never real."

She blinked hard, swallowing memories like glass.

"But for those months? I felt seen. Guarded. Loved."

Monroe's tone cut through the haze.

"Sometimes what disappears still leaves fingerprints."

Cam stared at her, searching, unsettled.

"I came today 'cause I didn't wanna be alone. And being here?" She rubbed her palms against her thighs, grounding herself. "It feels like the closest thing to home I got right now."

Monroe studied her. The way her hands shook, but her eyes stayed hard. The way her voice broke, but her Brooklyn spine kept her sitting tall.

Home wasn't just what Cam wanted.

It was what she lost.

And somewhere in the shadows of Brooklyn, Monroe knew, what Cam remembered as safety was the same presence Monroe now shared a bed with.

And that made the room colder than it had been a second ago.

MONROE'S JOURNAL

Monday | 6:00 p.m.

CLIENT | Cam | Session Two

Tonight hit me different.

Cam put something into words I've felt in fragments but never heard spoken aloud: that men fall in love with your potential, but they stay for the perks. She said it like a confession, but it sounded like prophecy.

And then, she painted a ghost.

She doesn't even know the name she whispered today. But I did.

Knight.

It was him. Or someone cut from the same cloth.

The details clung to her tongue like truth: tall, chocolate, Timbs in July, cologne too rich for the car he drove, protective without claiming ownership. Her Brooklyn Batman.

My husband.

Or his shadow.

I smiled through it. Nodded. Jotted my notes like I always do. But inside, my pulse was steady as a lie detector. Because how? When? Why would he never tell me?

Is it a coincidence, or a breadcrumb left in the rubble of his past, surfacing now with purpose?

Cam thinks she lost something after one summer. But what she doesn't know is that some men don't vanish; they reappear under new names. New lives. New vows.

This game is layered. More than therapy. More than confession. Every session feels like a door unlocking a room I never meant to enter.

And the deeper I go, the more I realize,

Even safety can carry secrets.

Tonight, I kissed his lips like I always do. Smelled that same cologne on his skin. But I tucked a new name into the folds of my memory.

Brooklyn Batman.

If she only knew.

And if I only knew the whole truth.

What else has Knight left behind for me to find?

—MH

CAM | OUTSIDE
Fulton Street | Bed-Stuy
Monday | 7:17 p.m.

The city always greeted her differently after Monroe's sessions. Like it knew what she'd confessed inside those four walls and wanted to remind her, nothing out here was safe enough to hold secrets.

Cam pulled her hood low, tugging the drawstrings tight. The heat was merciless, humid air pressing against her skin, but the hood wasn't about comfort. It was armor.

Fulton Street was alive, dudes in the hood popping wheelies on dirt bikes, corner speakers blasting drill too loud for the cracked subwoofers, a man selling incense and oils from his trunk trailing behind her: "Peace, queen, five for five, bless your spirit…"

She kept walking. Fast. Purposeful. Her gold earrings clinked when she moved, a reminder of who she was, Brooklyn to the bone, but carrying invisible luggage that only got heavier the longer she tried to ignore it.

Inside her head, Monroe's words replayed like a needle stuck on vinyl:

Sometimes what disappears still leaves fingerprints.

Cam bit her bottom lip. That summer had never let her go. The way Brooklyn Batman, as she'd named him, appeared out of nowhere, shadow and shield at the same time. He ain't hers, not really. But he was the only man who ever made her feel like home was portable, like safety could follow her down cracked sidewalks and broken streetlights.

Cam hated herself for still remembering the smell of his cologne when he leaned too close.

Her phone buzzed. A text.

"Pull up on Monroe. We lit."

Her cousin. The same one whose car Brooklyn Batman fixed.

Cam typed, "Bet," but didn't hit send yet.

Because that's when she saw it.

A black SUV. Tinted. Engine low, barely a growl. Parked at the far end of the block, just past the chicken spot. Same place where he once told a stranger she was "spoken for."

Her body went cold.

Coincidence? Maybe. Brooklyn was crawling with black trucks. But this one… this one felt patient.

Cam slowed her pace. Pulled out her phone like she was checking the time, though her eyes were locked in her reflection on the screen.

The headlights flashed once. Not a honk. Not a movement. Just one blink, like a signal. Then they cut off completely.

Her pulse roared in her ears.

She looked up. The SUV was gone. No door slam. No engine rev. Just gone, like it was never there.

Her throat went dry. Cars don't vanish. Shadows don't vanish. Men don't vanish. Not the ones who leave fingerprints behind.

She ducked into a corner bodega, heart hammering. The fluorescent lights hummed overhead, flickering once as if even they were in on the secret. She opened the fridge, grabbed a white peach Schweppes ginger ale, pressed the cold bottle against her cheek, and let it ground her.

Behind her, the bell on the door jingled. Heavy steps. She didn't turn around, just stared at the glass doors until her reflection blurred.

For a moment, she swore she caught a faint trace of something expensive in the air, oud, leather, smoke. The same scent from that long summer.

She blinked hard, shook her head. Too much therapy. Too much memory. Too much Brooklyn making her paranoid.

But as she left the store, ginger ale sweating in her hand, she couldn't shake the truth rising in her gut.

She wasn't just tired of being alone.

She was tired of being watched.

And for the first time since she was fifteen, she whispered under her breath, as if to herself, but maybe to the shadow that followed:

"Brooklyn Batman… if you're still out here, just tell me."

The night didn't answer.

Only the streets did, sirens wailing closer, laughter spilling from a dice game, the faint rattle of the Shuttle train overhead.

But under the noise, there was something else. A silence threaded too perfectly between the chaos. A silence that felt personal.

And Cam knew, Brooklyn wasn't holding its breath.

Brooklyn was watching her back.

JENX | SESSION TWO
Dr. Hunter's Office
Wednesday | 5:17 p.m.

The room felt different today.

Same plush chairs. Same Jo Malone candle, flickering soft shadows across the wall. Same glass desk catching the last gold slant of evening light.

But Monroe's energy had shifted. Focused. Sharper. The way the air feels right before thunder cracks.

She sensed it before Jenx even walked in.

Click.

Door closed.

This time, Jenx wore all black. Fitted, but not loud. No Céline shades masking her eyes. Just naked, unprotected pupils rimmed in charcoal. Her walk was slower. Intentional. A woman who'd seen something, or someone, since their last talk.

Monroe didn't rise. She didn't need to.

Jenx sat down, no greeting, no prelude. She looked Monroe dead in the eyes.

"I had a dream last night."

Monroe folded her hands in her lap, voice calm as silk. "Tell me."

Jenx's lips twitched like she had to force the words out.

"I was standing in my mother's old kitchen. The wallpaper was still peeling, those same little faded roses. And the smell, bacon grease. Like Norgate. Like childhood when hunger came dressed in smoke."

Her gaze dropped to the carpet.

"But she wasn't cooking. She was just... staring at the stove. Not moving. Not blinking. Just stuck. And I kept yelling her name, but she wouldn't turn around. She just kept whispering, 'Don't look behind you. He's still watching.'"

Monroe leaned in, tone velvet-smooth. "Who was she talking about?"

Jenx's jaw flexed. Her pulse jumped in her throat.

"I woke up before I turned around."

Monroe didn't blink. "But you already know who it was."

Jenx's stare locked on hers. A silence stretched long enough to break skin.

Then finally:

"Banks."

The name landed like glass on concrete.

Silence didn't just sit between them. It prowled like an unknown third presence in the room.

Jenx's voice dropped low. "I know something's off. Something I'm not supposed to see. But it's there. Right there. Like... like I'm walking through my life with someone else's shadow pressed against mine."

Monroe let the words settle. Then, softer, "What changed this week?"

Jenx shifted, shoulders squaring like she was bracing for impact. "I got a ping from his burner. The same location popped up three times."

Her eyes flicked upward. Bedford Ave and Clifton Place. Across the street from Rand's Liquor store.

Monroe's stomach flipped. Knight's block.

But her face didn't move. Not a twitch. Not a breath out of place.

Jenx didn't notice.

Or maybe she did.

Monroe's voice was steady. "Have you said anything?"

"To Banks?" Jenx's smirk was cold, practiced. "He lies better than he breathes. You don't confront ghosts, you study them."

"And what are you hoping to find?"

Jenx's mask cracked again. "Proof I'm not crazy."

Monroe inhaled slowly, exhaling through her nose, measured. "You're not."

Then she added, low and deliberate: "But paranoia is loyalty's grief. When you've loved someone beyond logic, even your mind mourns when the truth finally catches up."

Jenx blinked fast, like her body was trying not to feel what her spirit already knew.

She leaned forward, elbows on her knees, hands clasped tight like a prayer she didn't believe in anymore.

"I used to be proud of how much I knew about his life. Every move. Every call. Every number in his phone. Now? I'm scared I was only ever shown what he wanted me to see. A stage set for the fool I didn't know I was."

Monroe was still, but inside she felt the ground shifting.

"What do you want to see now?"

Jenx didn't answer right away. She chewed on the silence, weighing it like currency.

Finally, her voice cracked: "The truth. Even if it breaks me."

Monroe's gaze softened, but her words were knives wrapped in velvet. "Good. Because survival will cost you your soul if you're too loyal to what's killing you."

The room seemed to shrink around them. Candle flicker. Shallow breath. The hum of danger hiding in the walls.

Jenx stared into the floor, lips parted like she wanted to confess something else, but didn't.

"Next week," Monroe said slowly, "we're going to stop talking about Banks."

Jenx's head snapped up, brow arched.

"…and start talking about you. The woman who stayed. The one who knew. The one who's been quietly building an escape plan in the back of her mind."

Jenx froze. The words hit too clean, too precise.

Her lips parted. Her pulse beat hard against the thin skin of her throat.

"You don't know me," she whispered.

Monroe didn't flinch. "I don't need to. Your spirit already confessed."

And for the first time since she walked in… Jenx looked lighter.

Not safe.

But seen.

Like someone had finally caught the outline of the shadow she'd been dragging behind her.

And that made her dangerous.

Because a woman who feels seen when she's been invisible too long starts moving differently.

And Monroe knew it.

She didn't just have a client in front of her.

She had a live wire.

One that connected straight to Knight.

And the question wasn't if it would spark.

The question was when.

MONROE'S JOURNAL

Playlist: Can You Stand the Rain | New Edition
CLIENT | Jenx | Session Two

The older the client, the more expensive the mask.

But tonight... Jenx didn't wear one.

Not fully.

Not when she spoke about Banks. That woman's face. The numbness that followed.

That wasn't rage.

That was grief in a steel dress pressed, polished, and zipped up just tight enough to keep her from falling apart.

And I know it when I see it.

Because I've worn it, too.

She didn't cry. But I saw the flicker.

The war between dignity and devastation.

And that's always the deadliest fight when your pride is begging you to leave, but your soul still smells like his skin.

The real question under it all?

It's not "Does he love me?"

It's "Am I stupid for still loving him?"

That's where most women bleed out.

Not in the breakup.

But in the quiet courtroom of shame, where they're judge, jury, and defendant for feeling too much.

As New Edition played behind me,

"Storms will come... this we know for sure..."

I found myself wondering:

Can we stand the rain we caused?

Not just the storms someone else pulled us into...

But the internal downpours we invited by ignoring our own forecast.

Jenx isn't weak.

She's weathered.

She's been walking through emotional hurricanes in five-inch heels, holding everybody else's umbrella but her own.

And sometimes, the strongest women need the hardest storms to finally say:

"I'm done pretending I'm not soaked."

Next session, we won't talk about Banks.

We'll talk about the part of her that stayed.

The part that confuses pain with proof.

The little girl who learned love through sacrifice, and never unlearned it.

Because if she doesn't name it...

She'll marry it.

She'll mother it.

She'll pass it down in silence.

And one day...

She'll call it legacy.

— MH

JENX | OUTSIDE

Wednesday | 8:25 p.m.

Jenx didn't take the usual route home.

She walked... aimlessly... purposefully... both.

The moon was lit, casting that Brooklyn glow. The kind that made even cracked sidewalks look cinematic.

She reached Nostrand Ave. and slowed her pace as she passed Norgate. Her childhood whispered from its windows.

Her phone buzzed. Again. It was Banks. She didn't look.

She turned the corner and slipped into the tinted Benz parked halfway down the block. He was waiting, engine humming.

"You good?" he asked, not looking up.

"Yeah," she said, sliding in.

"How was ya little appointment?" he asked, mocking.

"It's not little. It's mine."

He smirked. Reached into the glove box and handed her a velvet pouch.

Inside, a diamond tennis bracelet.

"Here," he said. "Felt like you deserved somethin' nice."

She looked at the bracelet. Then out the window.

Something in her shifted.

And for the first time, a diamond bracelet didn't make her forget the ache.

PILLOW TALK

Wednesday | 11:15 p.m.

They lie in bed. Lights dimmed low. The hum of the fan in the corner spinning rhythmically into the silence.

Knight, one arm behind his head. Monroe rested on his chest. Her fingers tracing the tattoo near his collarbone.

Knight whispered, "You good, Halo?"

"Yeah… just tired. Long session."

"You always take on people's pain like it's your own."

Monroe forced a smile and, in a solemn tone, she said, "Maybe. But I'm built for this."

He kissed her forehead. That signature kiss that always makes her stomach flip.

"You're everything, Halo."

She smiled again. This one lingered… just a second too long.

Because somewhere between the warmth of his chest and the weight of her silence, Monroe was planning to remember everything.

BREADCRUMB

Monroe's Office

Thursday | 6:06 a.m.

Monroe arrived before sunrise. The air was too still, the streets too quiet, like Brooklyn hadn't woken up yet.

She unlocked the office, stepped inside, and stood still.

Everything looked normal.

But something felt... off.

The white orchid on the reception table was tilted two inches to the left. The hallway runner had one corner flipped just slightly. Her chair was an inch further from her glass desk than she'd left it.

She opened her drawer.

The contents were mostly untouched, except that her notepad was turned to a new page.

She hadn't done that.

And written at the top, in that same silver ink:

"Three came in. One left something behind."

Her throat tightened.

She checked the security feed.

Nothing.

The footage skipped from 10:13 PM to 12:42 AM. A two-hour blackout. Not corrupted, just... erased. Cleanly.

She glanced at the bookshelf behind her desk. Her psychology textbooks were aligned perfectly, as always, except one was upside down.

The 50th Law by 50 Cent and Richard Greene.

She hadn't touched that book in weeks.

She pulled it from the shelf. A Polaroid fell out.

Grainy. Dark. Blurry.

But the object in the frame?

Her office.

From the inside.

At night.

Taken by someone who had been here while she slept.

And in the bottom corner of the photo…

A blurry reflection of someone wearing oxblood stilettos just barely captured in the window pane behind her desk.

Her breath hitched.

She had only seen that shoe once before.

NAVI | SESSION TWO

Dr. Hunter's Office

Thursday | 8:01 a.m.

Monroe noticed the scent first. Oud for Greatness.

Not feminine.

Masculine.

Familiar.

"Morning, Doc," Navi said, sliding into the velvet chair.

Her voice was light, but her eyes had storm clouds.

Navi arrived early. Not the fashionably late entrance of a woman who commands time; this was different.

Intentional.

Weighted.

She wore a black Givenchy dress that molded to her like armor, sharp seams, clean lines, fabric heavy with silence. Oxblood crocodile Hermès Birkin at her wrist, swinging like a verdict.

"Morning," Monroe answered. "Who's here today, princess, queen... or someone else?"

Navi tilted her chin. "Checkers."

Monroe arched just one brow. "Explain."

"Chess is patience. Strategy. People with time can play chess. I grew up on reflex. Jump or get jumped. Checkers is survival."

Monroe's voice sliced through. "Reflex gets you across the board. Chess teaches you what to do once you're crowned. Queens don't just survive. They move the whole game."

Navi smirked, but it faltered. "Cute metaphor. But in checkers, all the pieces look the same until they're crowned. Nobody knows who you are until you survive long enough to earn it. I've been crowned my whole life for surviving."

"And what happens when surviving stops being enough?" Monroe pressed.

Navi's fingers clicked her rings against the chair armrest, rhythm betraying the truth her lips held back. "Then maybe I'm not the only player."

Monroe leaned forward, her voice velvet steel. "Then stop being a piece. Learn how to play."

For once, Navi didn't have a comeback.

MONROE'S JOURNAL

Thursday | 10:13 a.m.

CLIENT | Navi | Session Two

The rain hasn't stopped. Neither has the knot in my stomach.

Navi said "checkers" today, and I couldn't stop hearing Knight's voice.

'Checkers is for the block. Chess is for the world.'

And then the cologne, Oud for Greatness.

On her.

On him.

On everything I can't name.

Coincidence is lazy. This feels deliberate.

The therapist in me caught it the exact second she stopped performing. Her voice cracked. Her armor slipped. That's when I knew. She's not unraveling by accident. Somebody's pulling strings.

Which leaves me with two truths I don't want:

- Either she's been playing with him.
- Or she's been learning her moves from him.

And me? I'm realizing I'm not the therapist anymore. I'm a piece on the same board.

The Queen! The most powerful piece. Also… the most hunted.

Lord, don't let me fall.

Not to lies. Not to silence. Not to Knight!

— MH

NAVI | OUTSIDE

SoHo | Manhattan

Thursday | 9:23 p.m.

Rain turned SoHo's cobblestones into a chessboard, headlights bouncing across black-and-white squares.

Navi stepped out of Cartier empty-handed. The real power wasn't in the purchase; it was in leaving desire untouched. Her jet-black waves clung to her cheeks, mink brushing against Louboutin stilettos that cracked the pavement like verdicts.

And then she saw it.

The matte black SUV. Same corner. Same silence.

Her driver opened the door, but she froze. Queens don't flinch.

The headlights blinked once.

Not random.

A signal.

Her phone buzzed. Unknown number.

One word: WATCH.

She slid into the car, forcing her breath into rhythm. But in the tinted window reflection, her hazel eyes betrayed her. Not a princess. Not a queen. A pawn.

Chess, not checkers," she whispered, though her pulse didn't believe it.

BREADCRUMB

Dr. Hunter's Office

Saturday | 10:09 a.m.

Monroe hadn't meant to open the drawer.

She was reaching for a blank notepad when her hand brushed something else.

Not thick. Not heavy. Just… deliberate.

An envelope.

Black. Matte. No label.

It wasn't hers.

She never used stationery like that.

She froze. Picked it up.

Inside: a single note, written in silver ink.

The more you uncover… the closer it gets.

No signature. No name. No logo.

But the handwriting…

It looked familiar.

Not from therapy files. Not from Knight's notes.

It was the way the "g" curved at the end. The swoop is too long, like someone writing for style instead of speed.

Her stomach knotted.

This wasn't random. This was placement.

Someone had been in her office.

Someone with access.

She looked at the door.

Locked.

Checked the camera monitor.

Playback. Normal. Empty reception.

Except, a blur of oxblood leather.

Crocodile texture. Gold hardware.

The Birkin.

Two days ago.

Right after Navi's session.

Monroe had stepped out to take a call. Three minutes max.

The video resumed as if nothing had happened.

But Monroe knew better.

She replayed the clip.

Watched the timestamp.

8:47 a.m.

Three minutes.

Long enough to fold paper.

Long enough to open a drawer.

Long enough to set a trap.

Her heart thudded once.

She slid the envelope back into the drawer.

And for the first time in weeks, she picked up her phone and texted Knight.

Did you say Navi's name before I did?

No response.

Just three blinking dots.

Then nothing.

JENX | The Pullback
Saturday | 12:12 p.m.

Three days passed.

No calls to Banks. No pop-ups. No late-night check-ins.

She wasn't ghosting. She was recalibrating.

Instead of riding shotgun, she was riding solo in a borrowed Audi.

She wasn't plotting revenge. She was researching retreats.

Holistic ones. Tulum. Costa Rica.

She wasn't angry. She wasn't sulking. She was still.

And that scared him.

He video-called her.

She let it ring. Then declined.

"U good?" He texted.

"Yeah. Just taking care of me this week," she replied.

His response was simple:

"Bet. Hit me when you done."

No fight. No chase.

That hurt more.

JENX | The Reminder

Later That Night...

Jenx booked a solo table at Highwood in Weehawken.
She had just finished her mint tea when a familiar voice called out.

"Ayo... is that Crystal Jenkins?"

It was Ariana. Church girl. Usher board. Real friend!

They hugged long and loud.

They walked the waterfront.

"You happy, Jenx?" she asked.

Silence.

"I remember who I am," Jenx finally said. "But I don't think she likes it here."

Ariana pressed a silver cross into her hand.

"Just hold it. Even if you're not ready to wear it."

Later, Jenx stood in her bathroom in a black robe and charcoal mask, staring in the mirror.

Not the lashes. Not the lace front. Not the drip.

Just her.

In a low tone, she said, "I'm still here."

Jenx walked into the living room, quiet.

Banks was on the couch.

"You good?"

"Yeah."

"Where you been?"

"Weehawken. Dinner. Walking."

"With who?"

"A friend. One that remembers who I was before all this."

He stood. Tension rising.

"You tryna say you different now?"

"I'm sayin'… I remember who I really am. And I don't know if she likes it here."

She dropped the cross on the table.

Went upstairs.

Banks stared at it.

Then his phone buzzed.

"We need to talk.

— Her"

PILLOW TALK

Knight & Monroe's Home

Saturday | 11:17 p.m.

Soundtrack: "Sweetest Thing" by Lauryn Hill, playing low from Knight's vinyl shelf

The house was dark except for the faint spill of streetlight seeping past the blinds. Brooklyn was hushed, no sirens, no dice games, just the quiet hum that only comes after rain.

Monroe rested against Knight's chest, but her eyes were open, staring at the ceiling as if it held answers. He smelled like fresh soap and Oud for Greatness, his nightly ritual—always showering before bed, washing off the day before climbing under the sheets.

"You good, Halo?"

A whisper that could lull or unsettle, depending on the night.

She nodded against him. "Yeah."

But her mind was still in her office drawer, black envelope, silver ink, Navi's Birkin flashing across the monitor like a warning.

He kissed her temple. "Feels like you're somewhere else."

Monroe shifted, half-smiling, therapist mask intact. "Long day. Heavy sessions."

"You carry too much," he murmured, rubbing circles into her back. "Can't save everybody, Ro."

"Maybe I'm not trying to save everybody," she said softly, eyes fixed on his jawline, the way his pulse jumped when he lied. "Maybe I'm trying to make sure I don't miss the ones I'm supposed to save."

Knight went quiet. His thumb stilled, then picked up again. Rhythm controlled, like his breathing.

Monroe tilted her face up to him. "Did you ever say her name? Before I did?"

His brow furrowed slightly. "Whose name?"

"Navi."

Knight's expression didn't crack, but his silence did. It stretched long enough for her to feel the weight of every possible answer.

Finally, he kissed her forehead. "You dream too deep sometimes."

A deflection. Smooth. Brooklyn-slick.

Monroe smiled like she bought it. But inside, her therapist-brain scribbled a note she couldn't write down. *He didn't deny it. He deferred it.*

She curled tighter into him, playing the role of the safe wife, while her gut whispered like Brooklyn stoops after midnight: The game just changed. He knows I'm watching.

MONROE JOURNAL

Knight's Confession

Saturday | 2:07 a.m.

People think healing is a straight line. But healing?

Healing is a hallway with mirrors.

Some days, you walk right through.

Other days, you stop and stare at your own scar tissue.

Knight cracked open this morning.

And he didn't even know he was carrying the weight until the words came out.

He dreamed of his old self, the man he buried to become the man I married.

But the ghost still speaks fluent survival.

That shook me.

He said:

"I left the life, but did I leave the language?"

Whew.

It hit me like a client breakthrough.

Like that moment when someone finally says the thing they've been dancing around for six sessions.

Knight's love is deep, but it's been filtered through muscle memory. Protect. Provide. Power through.

Even in softness, he leads with coverage.

"Some men weren't taught to be vulnerable. They were taught to be useful. And when they fall in love, they show up as furniture: solid, dependable... and silent."

But not today.

Today, he let me in. No armor. No ego. No detours.

Just him, raw, reflective, real.

And he said something else, something I'll write on the sticky note for my desk tomorrow: "I've never loved someone who made me want to be known."

That? That's not just romantic.

That's redemptive.

Because it reminded me:

"Love isn't built on how loudly someone says they need you. It's in how safely they whisper their fears."

And the truth is...

We're all just trying to love someone without repeating the parts of our past that made it hard to love ourselves.

Knight reminded me today that even the strongest men still carry survival in their suit pockets.

But in this house?

We don't just survive.

We unpack.

We breathe.

We know each other.

Even the language we no longer speak.

— MH

CAM | SESSION THREE

Dr. Hunter's Office

Monday | 5:21 p.m.

Cam didn't sit right away.

She walked through the room like it was a crime scene. One hand brushed the spine of a psychology book. Another tapped the brass edge of a frame that read: "What you feel is not who you are. It's where you've been."

Her breathing was too shallow for safety. Her body was present, but her nervous system? Somewhere else entirely.

Monroe noticed. She noticed everything.

"Take your time," she said gently, keeping her notebook closed. "We don't have to start where you left off. We can start where you are."

Cam finally dropped into the velvet chair, but not like surrender. More like collapse. A quiet quake.

"My nervous system don't trust nobody," she muttered, "even when I do."

Monroe leaned forward slightly. "That's a powerful distinction. Who taught your body it had to stay ready?"

Cam looked at her, the mask slipping. "Life. But mostly, my mother."

Monroe let the silence stretch, then softened her tone. "Tell me about her."

Cam didn't speak right away. Her fingers were busy, wringing the drawstrings of her hoodie, folding and unfolding them like secrets.

"She cried behind closed doors and broke stuff in public. Left me to clean it up, both kinds."

She paused. "I was twelve, making bologna sandwiches for my little sister while my mother cried on the floor. Nobody asked if I was okay. They just handed me keys and told me to lock the door before dark."

Monroe nodded slowly. "That's the kind of survival that gets mistaken for strength."

Cam's jaw twitched. "You ever feel like your whole life was just prepping you to be left?"

Monroe's eyes didn't flinch. "Every abandoned child eventually becomes their own security system."

Cam exhaled hard. "And I don't know how to deactivate mine."

She sighed.

"I saw that SUV again. Same block. Same vibe. I felt it before I saw it. Same as last time."

Monroe raised her eyebrows slightly. "What did you feel in your body?"

Cam looked down. "Like my lungs shrunk. Like I was underwater. But the sick part? I didn't feel fear. I felt... wanted."

"That makes sense," Monroe said calmly. "When the only intimacy you've known came wrapped in inconsistency, even a ghost feels like home."

Cam sat with that.

"I don't want to be needed for my resilience anymore," she said. "I want to be loved for who I am beyond what eyes can see."

Monroe leaned in, voice precise.

"Then we have to find the version of you that believes she's worthy of peace even when she's not holding everything together."

Cam wiped a tear and whispered, "I don't know who I am without the weight."

Monroe delivered it like gospel:

"You are the person who's left after survival gets laid to rest. You're still standing." And this time, Cam didn't flinch.

She just nodded. Eyes swollen. Hands still.

Like something ancient had finally loosened its grip.

MONROE'S JOURNAL

Monday | 8:28 p.m.

Client | Cam | Session Three

Soundtrack: "Not Gon Cry" by Mary J. Blige (Waiting to Exhale Soundtrack)

The city outside my window always hums a little differently after a session like that.

Dumbo doesn't sleep. It simmers. The cobblestone streets outside my office are slick with August heat, the East River glinting like it knows all of our secrets and keeps them anyway.

Tonight, the windows are cracked just enough to let in the music of the neighborhood. Somewhere down the block, a live jazz trio is playing at that little wine bar on Washington. You can feel the bass line travel through the soles of your feet, straight up to the throat.

Cam sat across from me today, looking like a question mark dressed as an exclamation point.

Sharp. Beautiful. Uncertain.

When she talked about that moment in the car when she couldn't stop crying because her man didn't even notice she was breaking. I felt it.

Not heard.

Not held.

Not even seen.

Brooklyn builds strong women… but it rarely gives us space to fall apart.

"Not Gon' Cry" played softly in the background, Mary's voice pouring out like a diary we all wish we had the nerve to write.

"She's got to know that it's not her fault. She gave all she had, and he still walked… "

I had to close my eyes. Because somewhere in that song, Cam's truth unraveled mine.

How many times have I held myself together for someone who couldn't even say, 'I see you'?

How many times have we mistaken silence for strength?

Numbness for peace?

Or worse, love for loyalty?

That's what hit me hardest today.

Cam doesn't want to win at love.

She wants to stop losing herself inside of it.

And that ache…

That ache is older than her first heartbreak.

It's generational.

It's coded into the way we're raised to serve, fix, and forgive, until there's nothing left but the performance of being okay.

Cam wants to feel without falling apart.

To be held without having to audition for it.

To rest without being punished for being soft.

I see her.

And I know she's not alone.

So many women in this city walk into these sessions not to heal…

but just to survive one more day without disappearing.

Next time, we'll go deeper.

Not into the man.

But into the moment when she learned to stop expecting to be loved without earning it.

And when that day comes…

I'll make sure she knows.
The truth doesn't break you.
It frees you.

—MH

CAM OUTSIDE

Clinton Hill | Fort Greene Park

Monday | 10:09 p.m.

Cam didn't go home right away.

Instead, Cam drove the long way, windows cracked, wind curling through the car like it was brushing her edges. She needed air. Space. Distance from the version of herself she'd just exhaled in Monroe's office.

Courtney Berry's Unseen came on.

She didn't even realize she was holding her breath until the lyric dropped:

"They never see me crying. I try my best to smile all the time, but it feels like I'm slowly dying."

She increased the volume.

The sky over Brooklyn was bruised pink and lavender. Streetlights flickered like they were trying to remember something. And Cam? She was somewhere between memory and mourning.

She passed the old corner store on Greene Ave, where her mom once cursed out a stranger over a lottery ticket.

She passed the schoolyard where she used to fake being tough so nobody would smell the grief on her.

And then she pulled over.

Right by Fort Greene Park.

Hands shaking, chest tight. She threw the car in park and leaned her head back. The trees whispered overhead like they knew every secret she never said out loud.

"I just want someone to choose me...," she whispered, "without needing me to bleed for it."

The steering wheel blurred in her vision.

She wasn't the fixer tonight.

She wasn't the strong one.

She was just a woman unraveling.

And for the first time, she let herself come undone, in public.

Because healing doesn't wait for privacy.

It just wants permission.

JENX | SESSION THREE

Dr. Hunter's Office

Wednesday | 6:21 p.m.

Jenx didn't knock this time. She slid in like the door owed her entry. No frames. No shades. Just raw eyes rimmed red, like she'd been scrubbing memories all weekend and couldn't get the stain out.

She didn't sit. She stood at the bookshelf, back to Monroe, fingers grazing the spines.

"You ever feel like silence is louder than gunshots?" Jenx asked, voice steady but cracked at the edges.

Monroe leaned back, unbothered by the posture play. "Every day. That's why I burn candles, to remind me the light isn't optional."

Jenx finally turned, dropped into the velvet chair, and exhaled. The sound carried years.

"I heard Banks on the phone," she confessed. "He said a name. Real low. Thought I was sleep. 'Knight.'"

Monroe's pulse skipped, but her face stayed scripture-flat.

Jenx's smirk was bitter. "I ain't stupid. He don't talk names unless he's pressed. Said it twice. Like an address he ain't supposed to repeat."

Monroe laced her fingers together, resting them in her lap. "And how did it make you feel?"

Jenx laughed sharply, humorless. "Like I was standing in a room with no windows. Breathing somebody else's air."

Her voice dropped. "And maybe I been loyal to a man who ain't even loyal to himself."

Monroe let the silence expand until it pressed against both of them.

"Loyalty is only dangerous when it's blind. Yours isn't blind, Jenx. It's bruised. And bruises tell stories."

Jenx leaned forward, elbows on her knees, eyes cutting through the dim candlelight. "So what's my story? That I was smart enough to notice… but too weak to leave?"

Monroe's gaze sharpened. "No. Your story is that you were strong enough to build systems in chaos. And now you're brave enough to imagine what happens when you stop building for him."

Jenx froze, her breath hitching. The crack in her mask showed again, but this time it was wider.

She whispered, "I don't even know what I sound like without him."

Monroe leaned in. Voice velvet over steel. "Then let's find out."

The Jo Malone flame flickered. And for the first time, Jenx looked scared, not of Banks, not of Knight, but of her own reflection waiting on the other side of survival.

MONROE JOURNAL

Wednesday | 8:25 p.m.

CLIENT | Jenx | Session Three

Today, Jenx said the name "Knight."

Not as a suspicion. As a certainty.

I told myself, "Don't wear your feelings on your face." But inside, my entire body braced. Because secrets have a way of circling back through the people who never asked for them.

She thinks she's unraveling. She isn't. She's remembering.

The silence she carries isn't weakness; it's intel. It's the kind of silence women inherit when the men around them confuse power with fear.

She said she doesn't know what she sounds like without Banks. That is the most dangerous sentence I've heard in months. Because women who don't know their own voices are the easiest to keep captive.

I pushed her. Maybe too hard. But I needed her to say it out loud, that she has an identity outside of ledgers, codes, and loyalties.

And when she whispered, "I don't even know what I sound like without him," I realized...

I don't know if I know what I sound like without Knight.

The job is to hold mirrors. But today the mirror pointed back at me.

Jenx isn't just walking into my office with trauma. She's walking in with a map. And I can't tell yet if it leads to her freedom,

...or my undoing.

— MH

JENX | OUTSIDE

Gates & Nostrand | Norgate

Monday Night | 11:09 p.m.

The block was humming like a half-broken speaker. Dice popping by the hydrant. Kids riding bikes way past bedtime. Somebody's Bluetooth speaker blasting Biggie.

Jenx walked slowly, hoodie up, blending in but standing out. Every step pulled a memory from the pavement.

She passed Norgate, eyes drifting up to her old window on the third floor. Curtains different now. Voices new. But the smell, bacon grease and incense, still leaked into the night air.

Her phone buzzed. One word from Banks:

"Home?"

She stared at the screen, thumb hovering. Didn't reply. Slipped it back in her pocket.

That's when she felt it. Eyes.

She turned. Across the street, the matte black SUV again. Idling. Watching. Same faceless presence from the nights before.

But this time, the driver's side window rolled down two inches. Just enough for a hand to slip something out and drop it onto the curb.

Envelope. Black.

Jenx froze. The SUV pulled off, quiet as breath.

She crossed, crouched, and picked it up. No writing. Just a wax seal pressed with the outline of a knight chess piece.

She didn't open it.

Not yet.

But her chest tightened. Because deep down she knew, this wasn't Banks' move.

This was the board getting bigger.

And she was officially a piece.

THE CONDO, THE PAWN

The pawn sat there like it had been waiting for her. Matte black, no dust, no fingerprints, no explanation.

Her stomach dropped. The LuvSac still held the warm impression of her body, but her mind was sprinting.

No one had a key. No one knew this place.

No one was supposed to know. Not even Banks!

The matte gold ceiling shimmered above her like it was laughing. The shadows stretched long across the powder-pink walls, black squares slicing her sanctuary into a board she hadn't agreed to play on.

She set the Baccarat flute down, hand steady by force.

Fear was weakness.

Panic was surrender.

"Chess, not checkers," she whispered, as if saying it out loud could anchor her.

Her fingers closed around the pawn. Cold. Heavy. Too deliberate.

This was no accident.

This was a message.

At the window, her breath caught. The skyline glared back at her, glittering, merciless.

Then she spotted it, low, tucked between towers: a black SUV parked too long, too still.

Watching.

Waiting.

Jenx thought to herself:

Sometimes the move you don't make is still a move. Silence can be a strategy.

But silence can also mean surrender. Know which one you're playing.

The words rang louder than her pulse. She wanted to believe she was playing strategy. But, standing there, pawn burning in her pocket, skyline pressing in like judgment, it felt a lot like surrender.

She forced herself to step back from the glass, heart hammering, every nerve alive with the thought:

Whoever left the pawn… wanted her to know.

Not just that they'd been here.

Not just that they could touch her sanctuary.

But she was already in play.

The skyline across the water no longer looked like freedom.

It looked like an opponent: tall, gleaming, patient.

Every tower, every shadow, waiting for her next move.

NAVI | SESSION THREE

Dr. Hunter's Office

Thursday | 11:47 a.m.

Navi drifted in like a storm without thunder.

White silk trousers swayed at her ankles. Sleeveless Balmain blouse carved her frame into sharp edges, softened by fabric. Cartier bangles clinked softly, like prayers in disguise. Chanel N°5 lingered faintly, but the real shock was absence.

No wig.

No lashes.

No gloss.

Just Monique.

She collapsed into the chair, her posture still regal, but her energy cracked.

"I did something," she said. "Something that felt normal... but wasn't."

"Tell me," Monroe said.

"I drove to Clinton Hill. No brunch. No man. Just... parked. And cried."

The word "cried" landed heavy.

Monroe's voice cut the silence. "What does Clinton Hill mean to you?"

"Nothing. At least I thought. Then I found a valet ticket in my bag. Black envelope. All caps. Clinton Hill. No note. I don't remember going there."

Her laugh was brittle. "Sounds insane, right?"

"Not insane," Monroe countered. "Engineered. Someone wants you connecting dots."

"I wasn't curious until that ticket. Now I can't stop asking, why me? Why now?"

"And when you went?" Monroe pressed.

"Brownstones. Kids double-dutching, ropes smacking air like applause. A pit bull pulling its leash. And a man in a black SUV. Parked. Watching. Never moved. Didn't blink. I swear he looked at me like I was already catalogued."

Her lips trembled. "For the first time in years, I felt small. Like I wasn't Navi. Not the Hood Princess. Just a pawn."

Monroe leaned forward, voice sharp. "Checkers is reflex. Chess is strategy. But Queens don't win by waiting to be crowned. They win by refusing to be moved."

Navi's hazel eyes welled. "But what if I already am?"

"Then you stop being a pawn," Monroe said, steel threading her velvet tone. "Queens don't get played. They change the rules."

Navi's lips parted. And under her breath, almost prayerful, she whispered the lyric that had been haunting her all week:

"Today I wear a smile because I'm no longer where I was…"

"I want to believe that," she confessed. "But what if I'm still stuck?"

Monroe's voice turned tender but unrelenting. "Then we make sure you're not. Together."

MONROE'S JOURNAL

Thursday | 2:07 p.m.

CLIENT | Navi Blu | Session Three

Clinton Hill.

The SUV.

The envelope.

The silence.

Navi saw what I've seen. She thinks she's unraveling. I know she's being studied.

But what haunted me wasn't the car.

It was her whisper, Jules Juda's Movement.

"Today I wear a smile because I'm no longer where I was…"

She sang it like scripture. Not a lyric. A plea.

And that's when I realized: therapy is about listening for the crack. Today, she cracked. Not in her glamor. Not in her titles. In her truth.

Brooklyn raised us to jump first, ask later.

Checkers before chess. Reflex before patience.

But survival isn't the same as freedom.

Knight used to say, "Checkers is for the block. Chess is for the world."

But maybe he's been studying my moves all along.

Maybe Navi isn't my patient, maybe she's my reflection.

If Queens are the most hunted, then maybe my role isn't to defend the King. Maybe it's to flip the board.

So tonight I'll stop hiding.

And if this game is mine, then I'll play it.

Because Navi isn't the only one in motion.
We both are.

—MH

NAVI | OUTSIDE

Clinton Hill

Thursday | 11:24 p.m.

The block glistened after rain, black-and-white squares stretching like a chessboard under street lamps. Brownstones rose like watchful rooks. Steam from subway grates curled into the night. A corner bodega radio hummed faint Jay-Z.

Navi's SUV rolled to Kosciusko. She stepped out, draped in mink, heels slicing wet pavement into sparks. She lit a cigarette, not for smoke, but to steady her hands.

Then she saw it.

Same corner.

Same matte black SUV.

Her chest tightened, but her chin lifted. Queens don't flinch.

The passenger window slid down an inch. Shadow inside. Watching.

Her phone buzzed.

Unknown number.

Three words:

YOU'RE IN PLAY.

Ash scattered across her coat.

She crushed the cigarette under her heel.

And in her head, the refrain returned:

"I may have regrets, but He's not finished yet. I'm grateful there is… movement."

She stared at her reflection in the SUV's tinted glass.

No wig.

No gloss.

Just Monique.

Not crowned.

Not untouchable.

Just a woman asking God if He could still love her story.

Her lips cracked. "If I ever told my whole story… would anyone still love me?"

The SUV's engine roared to life.

The shadow didn't wave.

Just drove off, leaving her stranded on the board.

The Flashback

In a quiet drawer behind her favorite perfumes, Navi kept a Polaroid.

It was the last picture ever taken of her and her father.

She was five. He was suited, smiling, charming as ever.

She hadn't seen him since.

That same smile had drawn her to the one man she couldn't stop loving… even after he chose someone else.

She looked at the picture and whispered, "You started this."

Then she shut the drawer.

* * * *

That night, Navi opened her laptop and wrote an email she would never send.

Subject: Just In Case You Ever Wondered

I was the version of myself I didn't know how to be, for you.

I studied your silence like scripture.

I memorized your habits like poetry.

I prayed for your peace while choking on mine.

And when you left… you didn't just take love.

You took the parts of me that believed I was worth staying for.

She didn't cry. She hit save.

Then closed the laptop and let silence sit with her.

CAM | SESSION FOUR

Dr. Hunter's Office

Monday | 4:10 p.m.

Cam arrived like weather, you felt her before you saw her. Hair tucked into a low bun that wasn't trying to impress anybody. All-black fit: cropped hoodie, slim cargos, black Timbs tied tight. Gold hoops, no gloss. The kind of clean that says I'm here to work, not to be looked at.

She didn't sit; she paced the rug, counting stitches with her eyes. "I keep hearing him again," she said. "Not his voice, his absence. It hums." She stopped. "I know it's not love. But it's something that feels like... home."

Monroe held eye contact. "The body remembers patterns and calls them peace. Sometimes the nervous system prefers the predictable ache over the unfamiliar calm. That's not love; that's habit."

Cam's shoulders dropped a fraction. "So why do I miss danger?" she asked. "Why does 'don't have too much fun...' hit like a prayer?" The Jazmine Sullivan line hung in the air, five words that felt like a hand on the throat and a kiss on the forehead.

Monroe leaned forward, tone polished like a blade. "Because you were rewarded for endurance. You made suffering look easy, and people mistook that for strength. Let me be clear: endurance is checkers, fast jumps, and short-sighted. Chess is strategy, asking, 'What does this cost me five moves from now?'"

Cam sank into the chair. "I don't want to be a legend for surviving. I want to be boring, like... safe."

"Good," Monroe said, soft but surgical. "Define safe."

Cam blinked. "Honesty I don't have to beg for. Consistency that's not a performance. And a life I don't have to hide from."

Monroe nodded once. "Write it in the air with me."

She traced the letters:

H-O-N-E-S-T-Y. C-O-N-S-I-S-T-E-N-C-Y. V-I-S-I-B-I-L-I-T-Y.

She lowered her hand. "Now, the rule: if it costs your peace, it's overpriced."

Cam flinched like the word hit a bruise. "And the SUV?" she asked. "Still there. Same block. Same engine hum. I can't tell if I'm being haunted or handled."

"What does your body do when you see it?" Monroe asked.

"Shrinks. Then straightens. Then... hopes," Cam admitted, face hot with shame.

Monroe didn't blink. "That hope is the hook. We'll unlearn it. Between sessions, practice: three deep breaths, feet planted, name five things you see. Then ask, 'What's my move, not my reaction?' Queens don't sprint. Queens reposition."

Cam sat taller. "Queen as in...?"

"Queen as in you," Monroe said. "Not the fantasy he wanted to protect. The woman who doesn't need protection to be whole."

Cam nodded, jaw set. "Then today I choose boring. If boring is peace, crown me dull."

Monroe smiled, a precise warmth. "That's not dull. That's design."

MONROE'S JOURNAL

Monday | 5:05 p.m.

CLIENT | Cam | Session Four

Cam named a holy desire today: boring. In a world that praises spectacle and frames survival as sparkle, boring is blasphemy. Which is why it's sacred.

She laid out peace like a blueprint: honesty she doesn't beg for, consistency not staged, a life that doesn't require hiding. I told her checkers crowns you for running; chess crowns you for waiting. The Queen wins because she knows how not to move.

The SUV is still ghosting her streets. Headlights off, engine humming like a metronome of control. She asked if she was being haunted or handled. I heard the question beneath it: Am I being watched because I matter or because I'm easy to move? The moment she breathed, planted, counted, and chose, she answered herself.

There's something else I can't shake. The way Brooklyn keeps changing its clothes. The dice stoop becomes latte art; the bodega becomes a brand. The past is being pressure-washed off brick, but the bones still tell on themselves. Trauma's like that. Paint over it and it rises through the coat.

And then there's Jazmine Sullivan pulsing through it all. How a five-word warning can sound like prayer. Cam doesn't want the hook anymore. She wants the verse where the truth lives. Where you admit what you lost and keep walking anyway.

My phone lit up again tonight. The same silver dare: MOVE.

I set it face down and wrote instead: What if moving is refusing to run?

Queens are the most powerful piece on the board. If the game is shifting, my job is to teach them tempo, how to waste a predator's time by refusing to play fast.

In therapy terms, that's regulation. In Brooklyn terms, that's not giving the block a show. In chess terms, that's winning without touching a single piece.

And God, it was beautiful.

— MH

CAM | OUTSIDE

Fulton Street | Greene Ave | Fort Greene Park

Monday | 6:42 p.m.

Cam took the long way home. Earbuds in, Jazmine Sullivan's "Lost One" threading the city's pulse into her own. Taxi horns feinted, trains rumbled the bones of brownstones, and the gentrified glow of new cafés leaked onto the sidewalk like theater light. The old dollar store was a fragrance studio now. The bodega cat had a branded collar. A kid in a designer puffer zipped by on a scooter, right past the place her mom used to buy scratch-offs.

Cam cut down Greene Ave, the block where she learned to square her shoulders. The stoop where she fake-laughed through tears was now a short-term rental with keyless entry. A "Help Wanted" sign, barista, latte art required, flapped in a window where a hand-lettered "NO CREDIT" once yellowed with the sun.

Her phone buzzed. No name. Unknown.

WE SAW YOU TODAY. KEEP WALKING.

She stopped, pulse sprinting. The song kept playing, the five-word warning floating across the hook. She took one breath. Then another. Feet flat. Five things: streetlight, cracked curb, stickered sign, sleeping dog, her own shadow.

"What's my move?" she whispered. "Not my reaction."

She turned toward Fort Greene Park. The trees wore the last of summer like a secret. At the chess tables, two old men argued about a rook sacrifice, one shaking his head, the other smiling like time was the only opponent. Cam watched the board. How the Queen waited. How she didn't rush just because she could. Patience looked like power.

When she pivoted to leave, the matte black SUV slid past on the outer road, headlights off, windows too dark. It wasn't close enough to touch. Close enough to teach. She didn't flinch. She didn't follow.

"I'm not the one you move," she said, to the SUV, to the song, to her past. She took the earbud out, letting Jazmine's voice fade into leaf-noise, train-noise, Brooklyn-noise. And for the first time, the quiet didn't scare her.

TWO TRUTHS. ONE LIE.
Monday | 11:04 p.m.

The tub had gone quiet. Monroe's skin was still warm, scented with bergamot and Nashi Blossom, but her spirit was chilled.

Something shifted.

She heard the doorbell, the dip in Knight's voice... the way his chest stopped rising like it usually did when he was at ease.

He kissed her on the forehead. "Stay here. I got it."

She nodded, but her intuition grabbed her by the wrist.

Outside | *The Twin & The Flash Drive*

Knight stepped into the night, robe loose and untied, heart calm but on Go.

Sire leaned against the Escalade, arms folded, jaw clenched like he was holding back a storm.

"Why are you here?"

Sire held up a small black flash drive.

"She left this in my truck."

Knight's entire posture stilled. "Who?"

A beat.

Then: "The one you never talk about."

A vein popped out of his forehead. "You sure it's hers?"

"Same initials. Same silence. Same ghost."

Sire nodded toward the flash. "Said to tell you her past didn't die... it just got quiet."

Knight looked away, toward the street. The street he swore never to walk down again, metaphorically and literally.

"You think she knows where I live?"

Sire's silence was the answer.

* * * * *

Upstairs, Monroe moved.

Silently.

She grabbed her phone off the dresser and opened their private home surveillance app.

Front door cam: offline.

She tapped again. Nothing.

Except one flicker of audio…

"She never let go."

That phrase stuck to her ribs.

She toggled over to the hallway cam.

There he was, Knight, standing on the curb.

Arms folded. A man in all black with black Timbs untied standing in front of him.

Same height.

Same build.

She couldn't see his face.

A black flash drive exchanged hands.

No hug.

No dap.

No warmth.

Only weight.

Knight Re-enters

Knight opened the front door like a man with nothing to hide, but too much to explain.

He climbed the stairs slowly. Intentional. Controlled.

In the hallway, he paused. Took a breath.

In the bedroom, Monroe quickly closed the app, put her phone face-down, and adjusted her robe like nothing happened.

Knight walked in with the flash drive in hand.

Monroe greeted him with a soft smile. "Everything okay?"

Knight kissed her temple. "Yeah. Sire had something I didn't know I needed."

She nodded, catching his eye.

But her soul whispered:

Don't ask him tonight. He's still choosing how to lie.

They lay in bed.

Her eyes open in the dark.

His chest steady against her back.

The flash drive sat in the drawer beside him.

And in the drawer beside her... was the growing suspicion that maybe Knight wasn't the only one keeping secrets.

SAME SUV, DIFFERENT ENERGY

Dr. Hunter's Office

Tuesday | 1:12 p.m.

The black SUV had been parked across the street for 83 minutes.

Monroe knew this because she counted. Twice.

The matte black Range Rover looked just like Knight's… same model, same slick factory tint, same soundless presence.

But it wasn't his.

Knight was in Jersey.

Or so he said.

The SUV never moved.

No engine hum.

No rolled windows.

No visible driver.

It was still there when her twelve o'clock walked in.

Still there after her one o'clock canceled.

Still there when she took her tea to the front bay window. The one that faced Clifton Place.

Her gut began to pulse, that low beat only Brooklyn girls learn to listen to.

She grabbed her phone.

You outside? Monroe typed.

No response.

Not even the three dots.

Twelve minutes later, the SUV pulled off.

Slow. Quiet. Too quiet.

It didn't even hit the pothole on Water Street.

* * * * *

Later That Night

Del Frisco's Midtown | 8:26 p.m.

Knight showed up smelling like Tom Ford and purpose.

His hand sat low on Monroe's back as they walked in, like always.

He pulled out her chair. Ordered her drink before she even opened her mouth.

But when the valet returned his keys…

It was that SUV. Matte black. Seamless finish. Quiet wheels.

Monroe stared.

It can't be the same… right?

He smirked. "You looking at me like I forgot your birthday."

Monroe released a soft laugh. "Nah déjà vu. Were you outside my office today?"

"You asking if I'm stalking you or surprising you?"

She smiled, but inside, something shifted.

PILLOW TALK

Tuesday | 12:03 a.m.

The room was dim, lit only by the low amber glow of the salt lamp on Monroe's nightstand. The diffuser hissed softly in the background, filling the space with lavender and cedarwood. The kind of scent that made your shoulders drop without realizing it.

Monroe lay on her side, one hand tucked under her cheek, the other stretched across Knight's chest. He held her before she even asked. That's the thing about Knight; he reads her like scripture, with reverence. No rush.

Neither had said much since she got home.

He could tell she was still processing.

The truth stirred up in both of them.

Knight ran his hand slowly along the curve of her back. "You quiet tonight, Halo."

Monroe's lips curled faintly. "Been listening."

"To what?"

She tilted her head. "Myself. Finally."

He nodded, exhaling through his nose. "That's a loud place to be."

Then he pulled her closer, their legs intertwining beneath the weighted blanket. His voice dropped, almost a whisper.

"You wanna pray?"

Monroe nodded, eyes already closed. "Yeah... I do."

Knight shifted, cradling the back of her head in his palm like she was breakable, even though he knew better. His other hand covered her waist, anchoring her to the moment.

Then, he prayed.

"God... thank You for the woman You gave me.

For her brilliance, her boldness, and the battles she wins even when no one's watching.

Be her peace where she overthinks.

Be her rest where she overworks.

And God... be her mirror when she forgets who she is."

Monroe's chest rose sharply, then settled like the ocean at dusk.

She didn't speak.

She just tucked her face into his neck and whispered, "Amen."

Knight kissed her forehead, slow and secure.

"Ain't gotta be strong tonight, Halo. I got you."

She melted into him. No titles, no therapist armor, no curated poise.

Just Monroe.

Just held.

Just safe.

And outside, the city moved.

But inside this bed, the world stood still.

JENX | SESSION FOUR

Dr. Hunter's Office
Wednesday | 2:15 p.m.

Jenx walked in like the hood still had her on payroll, olive bomber jacket, black tank, distressed cargos tucked into black Timbs, untied of course, hood half-up. No lashes, no gloss. Just raw. Around her neck, a thin chain with a tiny flash drive charm.

She didn't wait for Monroe's invitation. She dropped into the chair like she was clocking in. "Doc, I don't dream much. My body too tired. But last night? It hit different."

Monroe leaned forward, notebook closed. "Tell me."

Jenx's voice lowered. "I was standing in Norgate, but it was split. One side still mine with cracked sidewalks, dice games, the corner kids that never grew up. The other side? Coffee shops. White strollers. Yoga mats. My block, but not mine."

Monroe nodded. "That's gentrification in real life, and your subconscious is showing you it in technicolor. You're caught between who you had to be, and who you're afraid to become."

Jenx's mouth twitched. "And there was a chessboard, dead center. Big as the street. Black pieces, white pieces, all set up. But the pawns, those were kids I knew. Dead ones. Ones who didn't make it past 18."

Silence. Monroe let it breathe.

"And when I looked up," Jenx whispered, "the Queen piece was me. But I was made outta glass. Every time somebody moved, I cracked a little more."

"That's your body telling you the truth. The hood crowned you for surviving. But crowns built on survival shatter when they're not reinforced with self-worth."

Jenx looked away. "Banks says the hood don't love you back, but he still expects me to ride like it does."

"Checkers loyalty," Monroe cut in. "You stay on the board until you're crowned. Chess loyalty? You understand the Queen ends the game. And sometimes the only way to win is to stop playing by their rules."

Jenx exhaled, long and shaky. "So what's my move?"

Monroe leaned closer. "Stop asking permission to protect yourself."

Jenx gripped the flash drive at her chest. "Then it's my move."

MONROE'S JOURNAL

Home Office

Wednesday | 5:05 p.m.

CLIENT | Jenx | Session Four

Jenx is all edge and exhaustion, but today she cracked. She admitted the dream, the block split between past and present, pawns made of kids she buried. And the Queen made of glass.

Glass Queens don't last. But the brilliance is she saw herself as one anyway. That means she knows her value. She just doesn't trust her durability.

Her whole life has been checkers, fast moves, quick flips, crowned only after you survive the board. But I told her what I know to be true: the Queen in chess is the most powerful piece because she redefines the game. She doesn't sprint; she controls tempo.

Jenx thinks Banks is love. But Banks is labor. She's been mistaking surveillance for intimacy and ledgers for loyalty. She doesn't see yet that her leverage is her freedom.

She left with the flash drive heavy on her chest, whispering lyrics from Courtney Berry's *Incredible*. "You're incredible! More beautiful than you know."

If she ever believes those words in her own bones, she won't need Banks. She won't need the SUV. She'll just be Jenx, the Queen who knows she can't be moved unless she decides.

But that's why she's hunted. Queens flip boards. And hunters hate nothing more than a woman who stops playing.

— MH

JENX | OUTSIDE

Gates & Nostrand | Norgate

Wednesday | 11:24 p.m.

The block wasn't hers anymore.

The corner store sold smoothies now. The stoop was scrubbed clean. None of it mattered. The ghosts were still here.

Jenx moved quick, hood low, black Timbs pounding the sidewalk. The chain around her neck hit the flash drive with every step. She gripped it tight in her pocket. Insurance. Protection.

Music leaked from a car stereo. Courtney Berry's Incredible. Not background tonight. A lifeline.

Don't let them tell you, you're not incredible…

She muttered it back. "Incredible. Even here." Her chest was tight. Her hands slick. But she kept moving.

Buzz. Phone lit up. Unknown Number.

TRADE. LEDGER FOR A NAME. MIDNIGHT. COME ALONE.

Her pulse spiked. Flight screamed *run*. Fight said *stay*.

She froze under the bodega awning, eyes darting. Fresh paint. Old tags bleeding through. SUV across the street. Black. Idling. Watching. Same one Cam saw. Same one Navi swore about. Same one Monroe felt.

Her stomach dropped. Legs wanted to bolt. She forced them steady. Hand on the flash drive. Breathe sharply.

"They're playing checkers," she said to herself. "I came to play chess."

And she pushed forward. Fast. Past the ghosts. Past the shine.

Straight into the dark, where the park and the game were waiting.

PILLOW TALK

Knight & Monroe's Home

Wednesday | 12:21 a.m.

The rain hadn't stopped since evening. Brooklyn streets hissed under car tires. Inside, Monroe lay against Knight's chest, but her body was still working. The therapist in her filing, cataloging, suspecting.

Knight smelled of soap and Tom Ford's Tobacco Vanille, the scent that once felt like home. His breathing was steady, but his grip around her waist was tighter than usual.

"You're quiet," he murmured.

Monroe kissed his shoulder. "Listening."

"To me?"

"To the city," she deflected.

Knight chuckled, low. "City never sleeps. But it don't always speak either."

She studied his face, how shadows from the window blinds cut across it like prison bars.

"Do you ever feel like people only see one version of you?"

His jaw flexed. "Every day. That's survival."

Her voice softened, therapist and wife in one. "Survival isn't love, Knight. It's checkers. Love is chess. It's not about staying alive, it's about building something worth living for."

He tilted her chin, eyes darker than the room. "And you think I ain't building that with you?"

Monroe held his gaze, smiling faintly, hiding the storm in her chest.

"I think you're building something. I just don't know if I'm the only one you're building with."

Knight didn't flinch. Didn't blink. Just kissed her forehead. Her gut whispered, "That wasn't denial. That was deflection."

BREADCRUMB

Dumbo Office Lobby

Thursday | 6:11 p.m.

The rain had started an hour ago.

Not a storm, just the kind of rain that drizzles sideways and soaks your ankles no matter what you're wearing.

Monroe exited the elevator, umbrella in one hand, keys in the other.

The lobby was quiet. Too quiet.

Jasper, the security guard who always greeted her with a dad joke, was nowhere in sight. His radio sat on the desk, crackling faintly. Coffee half-full. Steam gone.

Monroe paused.

She walked to the desk, peeking around the corner.

Empty chair. No sign of struggle. Just… absent.

She looked at the monitor above the desk. The lobby feed was looping still frames instead of live footage.

Weird.

She pressed the elevator button again, nothing.

Then she felt it.

Someone was watching.

She turned slowly.

A woman stood outside the building. Across the street. Perfectly still beneath a black umbrella.

She wasn't trying to hide.

But she wasn't trying to be noticed either.

Monroe couldn't see her face. Just the sharp silhouette, the high heels, the stillness. The kind that made time slow down.

And in her hand?

A manila envelope.

No label.

Just like the one from her desk.

Monroe didn't move.

Neither did the woman.

Then…

A black SUV turned the corner, headlights sweeping across the street.

The woman stepped backward into the shadows.

Never running, never rushing.

Just… gone.

Monroe stood there.

Frozen.

The elevator dinged behind her. Working now. As if nothing happened.

She stepped in. Pressed the button for her floor.

As the doors closed, her phone buzzed.

UNKNOWN

You're asking the right questions.

But not to the right person.

No name. No emoji. No trace.

She didn't reply.

But she saved the number.

And for the first time, she didn't feel safe in her own building.

THE WOMAN IN THE WHITE TRENCH

Outside Fulton St. Flower Market

Friday | 3:09 p.m.

Monroe needed air. She hadn't mentioned the SUV to Knight. Hadn't pressed Navi about the valet ticket. But both moments looped in her mind like a glitch in peace.

So she stepped out. Just a walk. Just some fresh-cut peonies from Miss B's Flower Cart.

As she reached for her wallet, a woman brushed past her shoulder, elegant, deliberate.

She wore a white trench coat with the collar popped and dark frames that masked her eyes. Her perfume smelled expensive... and familiar.

"You dropped something."

Monroe turned. The woman was already halfway down the block, heels silent against the pavement.

In Monroe's hand was a black envelope.

Heavy.

Velvety.

No stamp. No seal. Just her name in handwritten script.

Dr. Monroe Hunter

Inside, a single card. No return address. Cream stock. Raised gold lettering.

Just six words:

He loves you. But should you?

Her chest tightened.

She looked up. The woman was gone.

No cab door.

No turn into a store.

No trace.

Later That Night | Home

Monroe placed the envelope in her drawer.

Beneath a file marked: CLIENT INTAKE: ARCHIVE.

She closed it slowly. Locked it.

She kissed Knight goodnight like normal.

Laughed at his dry jokes.

Ate his favorite takeout on the couch like they did every other Saturday night.

But something had shifted. Not loud. Not obvious. She was watching now. Like the feds. Collecting clues in silence. Eyes open. Head on swivel. Heart braced.

NAVI | SESSION FOUR

Dr. Hunter's Office

Monday | 8:01 a.m.

The rain hadn't let up since 3:14 a.m. Not a storm, just that Brooklyn drizzle that seeps through collars and settles in your bones. The East River outside Monroe's window looked like steel under God's judgment.

Navi arrived on the dot. She always did. Today she wore ivory armor, a tailored Balmain trench coat over a black silk blouse, high-waisted trousers that moved like smoke. On her wrist? A Cartier Crash, rose gold, bending time like it owed her something.

She slid into the chair with her Hermès Birkin propped beside her like a bodyguard. Monroe noticed the scent shift, Delina mixed with a trace of Tom Ford's Tobacco Vanille. Knight had worn that on his coat two years ago.

"I didn't sleep last night," Navi confessed. "I had a dream. Felt like a memory."

"Tell me," Monroe prompted.

Navi's hazel eyes fixed on the window. "I was on a balcony in Monaco. White wine in my hand. But when I looked down, the glass had turned to blood. And when I stood up, my shadow didn't move with me."

Monroe let the silence stretch, then said, "Your subconscious is telling you what your conscience refuses to face. You're at peace... but something behind you is watching. The reflection doesn't lie."

Navi's lip trembled. "I don't know if I'm scared of what's behind me or scared of who I am without it."

Monroe leaned forward. "That's the difference between checkers and chess. In checkers, you keep leaping forward until you're crowned. In chess, sometimes the most powerful move is to wait. The Queen controls tempo, not by rushing, but by choosing."

Navi's smirk was faint. "So what if the game is rigged?"

"Then flip the board," Monroe shot back. "Queens don't beg for fair play."

For a moment, Navi looked almost small, the platinum waves replaced with fragility. Then she reached into her Birkin and pulled out a burner phone.

"This was on my windshield. Rang once. No number." She slid it across the desk. "I didn't answer."

Monroe didn't touch it. Her eyes stayed on Navi. "What do you think it means?"

Navi leaned back, voice flat. "That I'm not just being watched. I'm being studied."

MONROE'S JOURNAL

Monday | 10:24 a.m.

CLiENT | Navi | Session Four

Navi admitted her dream: wine turned to blood, shadow refusing to move. That's trauma's handwriting. The soul doesn't lie in metaphors; it bleeds in them.

I told her about chess. About how Queens don't chase crowns, they control tempo. She heard me, but fear was louder.

And then the burner phone. Left on her windshield. No fingerprints. No explanation. She said she's not just being watched, she's being studied. My gut says she's right.

Therapists are trained to separate projection from reality. But today, her paranoia felt like recognition.

When she left, the air in my office still felt occupied. My camera feeds show nothing. But my skin doesn't lie: someone else was there.

The city is playing checkers. But the board around us? That's chess. And if Navi is the Queen, then someone is setting the trap not for her, but for the hand that dares to move her.

— MH

NAVI | OUTSIDE

Madison Ave Penthouse

Monday | 11:27 p.m.

The city pulsed below like an erratic heart. Inside her penthouse, everything was curated silence: orchids blooming on schedule, marble swallowing sound, a record crackling faintly in the corner.

Navi poured herself a glass of Château Margaux, red staining crystal like prophecy. She tried to focus on the skyline, but her mind looped the balcony dream. Her shadow, not moving. The blood in her glass.

Her phone buzzed. A text.

UNKNOWN:

THE SHADOW DOESN'T BELONG TO YOU.

Her grip tightened. Across the room, her Judith Leiber python bag glinted in low light. She remembered Monroe's words: *Queens control tempo.*

She turned on the record player. Tonight it wasn't luxury jazz. It was *"Incredible."* The lyric landed like a dare: *Don't let them tell you, you're not incredible...*

Navi whispered to herself, "Even shadows can't dim me." But the wine glass shook in her hand.

When she glanced at the floor-to-ceiling windows, the reflection nearly stole her breath. The outline of a man, broad shoulders, still as marble, was behind her in the glass. She spun.

No one there.

But outside, on the street twelve stories below, a matte black SUV rolled slow, headlights off.

PILLOW TALK
Knight & Monroe's Home
Monday | 12:32 AM

Monroe lay across Knight's chest, his heartbeat steady as a metronome. The Jo Malone candle flickered low on the dresser. The rain had finally stopped, but her spirit hadn't.

"You're quiet tonight," Knight murmured, brushing his thumb along her arm.

"I'm thinking," Monroe said.

"About?"

"Shadows. Glass Queens. And how sometimes people study us like we're lab rats."

Knight chuckled low. "Baby, you overanalyze everything."

Monroe turned to face him. "Do you?"

His jaw tightened. He kissed her forehead instead of answering.

"All I know is, you're my peace. Don't let nobody rent space in your head."

She nodded, but her gut clenched. That wasn't reassurance. That was redirection.

THE CALL HE DIDN'T KNOW SHE HEARD

Upstairs Hallway | Their Home

Tuesday | 11:27 p.m.

Monroe wasn't trying to listen. She was walking barefoot from the linen closet, a silk bonnet in one hand, and a lavender linen spray in the other.

She moved slowly. The night was quiet. A storm had just passed, so the air felt washed.

Knight's home office was down the hall. Door cracked. Light dim. She didn't expect to hear anything, but she did.

"Nah, I told her it was nothing. It's handled. That part's clean..."

Monroe stilled.

"She don't know. And she won't, unless somebody talks. You good?"

Her hand tightened around the spray bottle. The lavender mist clicked inside.

Knight's voice dropped again. Lower. Slower.

"I know. I know what I owe. And I got it under control."

...

"If she finds out, it's gonna break her."

Monroe stood frozen in the hallway.

Not breathing. Not blinking.

She turned. Slowly. Walked back into the bathroom. Closed the door.

Set the bonnet down.

Sprayed the lavender mist like it could erase what she heard.

She looked at her own reflection and whispered,

What am I not supposed to find out?

THE PING

Waiting Room | Monroe's Office

Wednesday | 2:07 p.m.

Knight had dropped off Monroe's favorite lunch: a kale salad with salmon and strawberry lemonade from her spot in Fort Greene.

He kissed her cheek. Told her to eat.

Said he was headed back across the bridge for a meeting.

Thirty minutes later, her tablet pinged. Family Location.

Knight's location said: Adelphi.

That wasn't downtown. That wasn't his meeting.

That was her neighborhood. Clinton Hill.

Blocks from her old high school.

Three from where her father used to take her to the bodega after church.

She stared at the red pin. Heart thumping.

Why would Knight be in her old neighborhood when he said he was going to the city?

She double-tapped. It hadn't updated in twelve minutes.

Then the pin disappeared.

Location Unavailable.

MONROE'S JOURNAL
Wednesday | 11:15 p.m.

Dear God,

Why does it feel like everything is whispering and nothing is speaking?

He holds me so close, but something feels… farther. I want to believe what I see: the man who kisses my forehead, who rubs my feet, who tells me I'm his center.

But then I hear the call. I see the envelope. I catch the scent on a stranger.

Is it me?

Is my past catching up?

Or is it his?

I can't tell yet.

But I'm listening.

And I'm watching.

Lord, don't let me misjudge love.

But don't let me sleep through a warning.

– MH

PILLOW TALK

Wednesday | 1:07 a.m.

The sheets are fresh, lavender-scented, and tucked tight. The Nashi Blossom Jo Malone candle flickers on the dresser.

Knight is on his back, one hand behind his head, the other scrolling through something on his phone. Monroe is beside him, under the covers, staring at the ceiling.

He glances over.

"You good, Halo?"

"Yeah."

"You sure? You been quiet."

"Just a long day."

Knight puts his phone down. Turns toward her.

"Talk to me."

"I can't tonight."

Knight leans in, studying her face. "What's going on in that beautiful head of yours?"

She turns to face him, forces a smile.

"Honestly? I just want to lay here. In this moment. Pretend like I'm not thinking."

Knight nods, kisses her forehead. "Then we'll just lay here."

He pulls her closer. Arm draped across her waist. Protective. Familiar.

But this time, she doesn't fall asleep. She's wide awake. Every breath he takes, every twitch of his fingers… she records it.

Because Monroe Hunter is no longer guessing.

She's building a case.

And the man in her bed?

Might be at the center of it all.

A PING BEFORE PEACE

Monroe's Loft

Thursday | 5:05 a.m.

Monroe woke up before the sun. Not because of a sound. But because something felt… off.

Knight's arm was draped around her waist, his body warm, breath even.

He was still asleep.

But her phone wasn't.

A faint blue glow pulsed from the nightstand. Silent. Intentional. She reached for it carefully, trying not to wake him.

1 Missed Location Ping 3:47 AM

Knight's AirTag: Clifton Place & Nostrand

She stared at the screen.

That wasn't the gym.

That wasn't anywhere near the gym.

And that definitely wasn't anywhere he said he'd be.

Her thumb hovered over the message.

Just a location.

The address where Knight grew up.

A street he rarely spoke about.

A street he swore he hadn't set foot on in years.

Monroe glanced back at him.

He looked so peaceful.

Too peaceful.

She slipped out of bed like a whisper, barefoot on the hardwood, careful not to step on the cold creak in the floor by the closet.

Wrapped her satin robe tight. Moved to the kitchen and opened the drawer where she kept nothing but batteries, pens,

and now a folded black envelope.

It had arrived last week.

No name. No stamp.

Delivered by hand.

Inside: one sentence.

He only hides what he loves most.

She hadn't told him.

She hadn't told anyone.

Her therapist's mind raced with possibilities…

But her heart? Her heart begged her to breathe.

To not jump to conclusions.

To not turn love into a case file.

But she knew better.

Love was blind, but instinct always had perfect vision.

She looked back down at the ping.

Clifton Place.

At almost 4 a.m.

The same place she'd seen on a valet stub in Navi's Birkin just days ago.

The walls weren't closing in.

They were shifting.

Quietly.

Intentionally.

And Monroe? She was starting to move like the feds, collecting data in silence. Watching patterns. Connecting dots.

She would not confront him.

Not yet.

Instead, she texted herself one word:

Clifton.

Then she slipped back into bed like nothing happened, curling into Knight's chest.

His hand instinctively pulled her closer.

She closed her eyes.

But sleep never came.

MONROE

Dumbo, Brooklyn | Therapy Office

Thursday | 7:04 a.m.

The city moved slow this morning. Not because it was tired, but because it was watching.

There's a silence in Dumbo that only the river understands. It doesn't rush. It rolls. Steady. Patient. Dangerous.

Monroe unlocked the front door to her office like a ritual, two slow turns of the key, one measured breath, then inside.

The space always smelled like Nashi Blossom and glass ambition. Every detail was intentional from the handblown vases on the corner shelf to the suede accent chair no one sat in unless they were ready to tell the truth.

She didn't play music yet. Not today. The silence was saying more than any Marvin Gaye record could.

Her heels echoed across the floor. She paused by the mirror, a quick scan, not for vanity, but for control. Hair in place. Eyes sharp. Edges laid. Armor, secured.

But inside?

Still unsteady.

Jenx's last session left an aftertaste. Like whiskey after communion, something holy, but hard to swallow.

Monroe slipped off her coat and hung it beside her long beige trench, Knight's favorite. Said it made her look like she was on the cover of a James Baldwin novel.

She smiled at the memory… but the warmth didn't last.

Something had shifted in the air.

Her favorite candle on her desk was untouched from last week. Normally, she'd light it before her first session, a soft start to sacred ground. But today, she hesitated.

It wasn't fear. It was intuition.

Something. Someone was coming.

And she needed to see it clearly.

She sat down slowly, crossed her legs, and pulled out the notes from Navi's last session.

That fragrance, Oud for Greatness, still lingered in her memory.

So did the silence after Navi said, "I've run out of places to pretend I'm okay."

Monroe flipped to the next page in her planner. A small scribble she hadn't written.

A date.

A time.

Nothing else.

Friday. 6:23 p.m.

Her pen hadn't made that mark. She never used blue ink.

She looked up at the camera in the corner.

Red light: off.

JENX UNSCHEDULED VISIT

Dr. Hunter's Office

Friday | 2:14 p.m.

Jenx walked in slowly. Hoodie pulled low, shades on. She looked like a storm had passed through her body, but left her standing.

Monroe didn't speak.

She just stood, gave a warm nod, and motioned to the couch.

Jenx sat like she was afraid the cushions might shatter her. "I ain't come to talk. I came to... unload."

"Unload everything you need."

Jenx pulled a photo from her pocket. Her fingers trembled.

She laid it down like it was a weapon she'd carried too long.

It was faded.

A block party.

Banks posted up in a yellow Coogi and gold fronts.

But behind him, partially blocked, was a tall man in black.

Sharp jaw. Waves. Durag.

Timbs laced halfway. Eyes hidden.

On the back, a handwritten label. *Norgate Crew | Gates Ave, Summer 2007*

"That's him. That's who Banks always deferred to. Never called him by name. Said, '*The Quiet One moves different.*'"

Monroe kept her breath shallow.

Jenx softly, "You ever hear of Knightmare?"

Monroe blinked slowly. "Why?"

"That was his street name back then. I only heard it whispered once, when they thought I was asleep on the couch. Said he cleaned up messes. Made people disappear. But he ain't move like no monster. He was... quiet. Calculated. Banks looked up to him. Almost feared him."

Monroe stayed still, but her pulse was sprinting.

"I don't know why I brought this. Maybe to remind myself that the man I loved was never the top dog. He answered to someone. And I was just the bookkeeper with a pretty face."

She sniffled and removed her sunglasses.

Her eyes were swollen, but fierce.

Jenx confessed, "I stayed because I thought I could be the soft spot in a hard man's life. But all I became was another business asset. He had me doin' payroll, hiding money. I never touched the drugs, never smoked, never sipped Henny, but I was in it."

"And when did it start to feel like prison?" Monroe pressed.

"When I realized I couldn't leave without feeling guilty for his downfall. Like if he went down, it was my fault."

Monroe walked to her. Kneeled.

Same height, same pain.

"You sacrificed your future for his illusion of control. But Jenx, your freedom doesn't owe him anything."

Jenx looked into Monroe's eyes.

"Why do we love the ones who chain us the tightest?"

"Because we think if we're strong enough to love them right... they'll never leave.

But love without freedom is not love. It's ownership."

Jenx started crying. Loud, choking sobs.

Monroe didn't stop her. Didn't rush it.

Finally, Jenx whispered, "He told me once, the only person he feared was the one who taught him silence. Said that man saved him... and ruined him."

Monroe, still grounded, said nothing. But her soul screamed. She'd heard similar words from Knight.

Jenx asked, "You ever wonder if your protector might've been somebody else's predator?"

Monroe closed her eyes.

And in that silence, she felt God stretch her heart wider.

"I'm done."

Monroe stood, helped her up, and said the only thing Jenx needed to hear,

"You're free now."

MONROE'S JOURNAL

Friday | 4:18 p.m.

CLIENT | Jenx | Unscheduled Visit

There are moments in therapy where the silence after someone speaks feels louder than a scream. Today was one of those moments. Jenx looked me in my eyes and said, 'You ever wonder if your protector might've been somebody else's predator?'

She didn't flinch. She meant it. And the worst part is, I understood it. Therapists are trained to hold space. To create room between what we feel and what our clients feel. But today... that space collapsed. Her words crawled up my spine and whispered directly to my fears. It's humbling when your client becomes your mirror.

I teach women how to reframe pain. I teach them to trust their gut, to identify the patterns that keep them stuck in survival. But what happens when my gut is yelling and I'm too afraid to listen?

The truth is, Jenx is grieving not just the loss of a man, but the loss of who she was willing to become for that man. That's a different kind of death. The kind that haunts you in the mirror every morning. I sat across from her and realized: my job is not just to help women find freedom. It's to help them forgive themselves for staying too long.

Today's session taught me that silence doesn't always mean healing. Sometimes it's protection. Sometimes it's trauma dressed in maturity. And sometimes... it's fear.

Jenx's photo rattled me. Not just because I think it's Knight.

But because I don't want it to be.

This work. This sacred work of healing has always been about building bridges between who you were and who you're becoming. But what if that bridge leads to someone you thought you already knew?

I keep saying I'm fine. That I'm focused. That my life is whole.

But I'm not. Not right now.

Because every time I look at Knight, I see the man who loves me. And every time I blink, I wonder who else remembers him differently.

– MH

PILLOW TALK

Friday | 12:26 a.m.

The bedroom was dim, lit only by the soft flicker of a Jo Malone Wild Bluebell candle. The scent danced through the air, sweet, sharp, clean.

Monroe lay on her side watching Knight.

He was fresh out the shower, smelling like Tom Ford and secrets.

He slipped into bed, his waves still damp, Timbs now tossed by the door like armor unstrapped. His bare chest was warm as he pulled her in, resting her head beneath his chin.

"Rough day, Halo?"

He always called her that. Said she looked like a quiet storm sent from heaven the first time he saw her walk across the gala stage in white.

"Yeah. A client came in today."

"Lil' firecracker?"

"Yeah… she left a piece of herself on that couch."

Knight nodded. He didn't pry.

Never did.

He respected the boundary of her work, but tonight, Monroe wished he'd ask. Because in the silence, her mind spun.

Knight's grip tightened ever so slightly.

Protective. Familiar.

But Monroe's eyes drifted to the edge of the dresser.

A folded note she hadn't thrown away. A black envelope in her nightstand drawer. A picture in her purse.

Knight kissed the side of her face. "You smell like questions." Knight smirkingly stated.

Monroe chuckled lightly. "You always read me."

"'Cause you ain't slick."

She studied his profile.

Sharp lines. Deep-set eyes. A jaw that softened only for her.

She searched for anything, anything, that looked like guilt.

But all she saw was her man.

"You thinking too hard, Halo. You need to let your mind rest. It's just me and you in here."

He wrapped his arm around her waist tighter.

The safety of it made her ache.

"You ever wonder if people see you differently than you see yourself?"

Knight looked down at her. He didn't flinch.

"Every day."

He leaned in and kissed her shoulder.

"But I don't live for their memory. Only yours, " Knight responded.

Her eyes burned.

He always knew what to say.

That was the problem.

Knight reached for the remote. "Let me play you something."

"Roni" by Bobby Brown filled the room.

He mouthed the lyrics, off-key but intentional.

Monroe smiled. She couldn't help it.

"That's you. My tender Roni."

She closed her eyes.

She wanted to believe it.

Wanted it to be only this music, his warmth, his Brooklyn laugh rumbling in her ear.

But in her mind, the couch still held Jenx's tears.

And the picture still whispered, *Knightmare*.

Monroe lay still, collecting evidence in silence.

Holding him close. Keeping her eyes open.

And her heart, guarded.

KNIGHT'S TRUTH

Friday | 2:04 a.m.

It all started with a phone call.

Blocked number. 2:07 a.m.

Knight was in the kitchen, shirtless, leaning against the marble countertop with a cup of hot ginger tea, Monroe's favorite.

She was asleep.

Or so he thought.

He answered with his usual calm.

"Go."

The voice on the other end said only three words.

"She's asking questions."

Knight didn't flinch. Just stared out the kitchen window at the matte black SUV parked beneath the streetlamp.

He hung up.

Opened a drawer behind the spice rack and pulled out a black envelope identical to the one Monroe had hidden.

Inside was a photo.

An old one.

Jenx. Back when she wore Baby Phat jackets and lip gloss thick as glass. Knight with his arm around her brother, Ty.

The original Norgate Crew.

Gates & Nostrand.

Bed-Stuy royalty.

Banks wasn't the only one who had stripes.

Knight had kept his past quiet, not because he was ashamed, but because Monroe didn't need to carry it.

What she didn't know was that he helped fund Banks' early moves.

Not out of ambition.

Out of protection.

Ty had been like a little brother.

When he got caught up and disappeared, Knight stayed close to Jenx.

A silent guardian.

The night she almost got caught in the crossfire, it was Knight who snuck her out the back door and sent her to live upstate for a year. She never knew who made the call. But she'd never forget the man in the Timbs who told her to run.

Then there was Navi.

That wasn't supposed to happen.

She reminded him of someone he had lost. Someone soft and always smiling.

For two months, they had dinners in dark corners of the city.

He never took photos.

Never gave his last name.

He just needed someone to remind him he wasn't all war and weight.

But then Monroe walked into his life with that stormy silence. With her all-white power suits and her broken-but-still-standing heart.

He knew she was it.

He changed everything for her.

Left the crew.

Got legit.

Used his connections to help veterans, single moms, and displaced men find footing.

Knight was the muscle… with the mission.

An email came from an encrypted server.

Subject line: *TRUTH.*

Attached were three audio files.

One from Jenx.

One from Navi.

One from Cam.

Each one unknowingly confessing the same man had touched their lives.

Each one unknowingly speaking about him.

He closed the laptop, his chest rising.

He had tried to bury the past. To reform the man he once was. But the past wasn't just knocking. It had built a house on the same block.

The final blow?

The mystery woman.

Her name was not a mystery at all.

Simone LaRue.

Former fiancée.

The only person who had ever made him question Monroe.

She was back.

Not for love.

For leverage.

Knight had made a mistake. Years ago. A deal. A favor.

One that led to her brother getting knocked.

She blamed Knight. Always had.

Now she was watching Monroe.

Sending photos.

Planting seeds.

She wanted Knight to come back to the darkness. Or lose the one thing he'd fought to protect.

His peace.

His Halo.

Knight took a deep breath.

Tomorrow, he'd tell Monroe everything.

Tonight, he'd hold her a little closer.

Because come morning, the truth would break the world they built together.

And somehow, he had to pray…

It would rebuild something stronger.

MONROE'S JOURNAL
Friday | 4:01 a.m.

The silence tonight is so loud it's humming.

The candle flickers on my nightstand, casting soft shadows that dance against the wall, like ghosts who know the ending before I do.

I watched him brush his waves earlier, caught the way he stared at himself just a second too long in the mirror. Like he was rehearsing. Like he knew he was about to lose something... or someone.

When he climbed into bed and pulled me close, his hands were warm. Familiar. But they felt like they belonged to someone I hadn't met yet.

And me?

I lay there, back against his chest, pretending to breathe normally.

Pretending I wasn't clocking every move.

Pretending I hadn't memorized every lie.

I remember being eight years old, sitting on the stairs past bedtime, watching my father leave the house with a fresh white tee and excuses dripping from his cologne.

My mother didn't say a word.

She just folded laundry.

Her silence was ironclad.

Now I understand...

It was armor.

Tonight, I wear that same armor.

Not because I'm strong.

But because I'm breaking.

I smelled my favorite perfume on that note. *Queening* by Mind Games.

Knight introduced me to it, and I love it as much as I love him.

But why? How?

Does this mystery person know me or Knight?

My mind can't help but wonder.

I've seen the black SUV three times this week.

Once outside the office.

Once across from the gym.

And tonight? Parked down the block from our building.

I know.

And Knight knows I know.

But we're dancing.

Two professionals.

One trained to protect.

One trained to observe.

He whispers 'Halo' in my ear like it still lands the same.

And it does.

That's what terrifies me.

Because I still want him.

Still crave the way his swaggy Brooklyn accent wraps around my name.

Still melt when he puts his hand on the small of my back in public.

Still watch how he watches me, like I'm his favorite secret.

But I don't know if I'm his cover story… or his collateral damage.

Cam. Jenx. Navi.

They were never supposed to overlap.

Their stories weren't supposed to intertwine with mine.

But here we are.

One black envelope.

Three sessions.

One man.

And me, caught in the crossfire between what I know as a therapist… and what I fear as a woman.

Tomorrow, I ask the question I've been dreading:

'Knight, who are you?'

And if he answers me honestly, I don't know if I'll survive it.

The worst part?

I still love him.

I still want to believe there's a version of the truth where he did it all to protect me.

That all of it, the silence, the distance, the misplaced glances, were sacrifices made to keep me from a world I never asked to enter.

But I'm already in it.

Neck-deep.

Wrapped in whispers and timelines and questions I don't even know how to ask.

I've been the therapist.

The fixer.

The woman with the answers.

But now I'm the one unraveling.

How do you look the man you love in the eye, knowing he's the reason the ground beneath you is cracking?

He says, "I got you," like it's scripture.

But right now, all I feel is weight.

I don't know if I'm the cover… or the consequence.

Tomorrow, I face the truth.

Not just his.

But mine too.

Because maybe… just maybe…

I stayed silent because deep down, I knew.

And if I knew, and still chose him, what does that say about me?

God help me.

Because tomorrow… everything changes.

– MH

THE STILLNESS BETWEEN SUSPICIONS
DUMBO | Brooklyn
Monday | 9:33 AM

The office smelled like fresh jasmine. Monroe had finally lit the candle.

Not her usual Jo Malone.

She chose something softer. More nostalgic.

Something her grandmother used to burn when the weather changed and prayers felt heavier.

She sat on the edge of her chaise, shoes off.

Still.

But not calm.

Her mind was running reroutes around every blink.

That bag.

That cologne.

That envelope.

And now?

That flash of oxblood outside the monitor two days ago.

That same scent clinging to Navi's session like a shadow.

She rubbed the bridge of her nose.

This wasn't paranoia.

She knew better.

This was intuition sharpened by a thousand women's confessions.

And now, it was her own soul whispering: "Pay attention."

She glanced at her security feed again.

Paused the footage.

Zoomed.

There.

Navi reached into the Birkin at 8:28.

 Looked at Monroe's desk.

Stood up. Tilted slightly to the right, just enough to block the view.

The camera caught only a sliver.

But Monroe could feel it in her bones.

Navi had placed the envelope.

Why?

Why that drawer?

Why her?

Monroe tapped her phone.

No new messages from Knight.

Still nothing.

Still those three dots blinking like a stalled heartbeat.

Her eyes scanned the room.

Everything in place. Her diploma. Her degrees.

A small velvet chair for clients who needed softness.

And one that sat lower for those who needed grounding.

But for the first time since opening this practice, Monroe felt like she was sitting in someone else's story.

She wasn't in control.

She wasn't one step ahead.

She was mid-page… in someone else's plot.

And whoever was writing it knew how to twist the pen.

She rose from the chaise.

Crossed the room barefoot.

Opened her drawer.

She blinked.

Once.

Twice.

Gone.

She spun toward her desk camera. Checked the live feed.

Nothing.

But when she turned back…

There, on her glass desktop, was a different note.

Still black paper.

Still silver ink.

But shorter.

Not everything you call intuition is safe.

And that's when the lights flickered.

Just once.

Like a warning.

Like a line being crossed.

Monroe backed up slowly and whispered.

Not a prayer.

Not a scream.

Just a name.

"…Knight."

WHAT KNIGHTMARES ARE MADE OF

Flatbush Avenue | 3 blocks from where it all started

Tuesday | 10:10 a.m.

People know him as Knight.

But only two people on Earth remember what it used to be short for.

Knightmare.

Because by the time you realized he was on your block, you were already living your worst one.

Malik Woods never chose that name.

The streets gave it to him.

Back when the only light he saw was from a Bic lighter flicked beneath a cracked spoon.

Back when he wasn't protecting people, he was collecting.

Back when the only justice came with silence, and loyalty was a handshake backed by steel.

But today…

He walked like a ghost from that life, clean, covered, and undeniably Brooklyn.

Black hoodie.

Dark jeans.

Untied black Timbs, creased just right, no scuffs, like he never ran from anything in his life.

He turned the corner onto a block that should've been condemned ten years ago.

They were renovating now. Cafés and murals where bodies used to drop.

Gentrification had a short memory.

But Knight didn't.

He passed the barbershop, an empty chair where OG Rich used to cut.

Passed the bodega, new owner, same bullet holes behind the Lotto sign.

And then he stopped.

There it was.

The wall.

Still tagged with his first name, *KNIGHTMARE.*

Faded but there.

He ran his hand across it.

"Still breathing," he whispered.

Then his phone buzzed.

A message. From a contact labeled only:

K.R. DO NOT RESPOND

You made a promise. I kept your secret.
But she's asking questions you can't afford to answer.
Meet me where it ended.

He didn't blink.

He didn't reply.

He just stared at the wall one more time...

Then walked.

Not toward the future.

Not toward the past.

But toward whatever was about to show up uninvited.

MONROE'S JOURNAL

Tuesday | 3:04 AM

Playlist: "All Night Long" SWV |Waiting to Exhale Soundtrack

The minute I walked into my office, I hit play on my late-night playlist. SWV's "All Night Long" whispered through the speakers, warm, velvet vocals curling around the silence like a slow dance I didn't ask for.

Knight had been gone all evening. No explanation. Just a forehead kiss at 7:00 and "I'll be back before you blink."

I blinked.

He didn't come back.

And now, the stillness in my office felt heavier than usual, like the walls knew something I didn't.

There's a scent on his jacket. Not cologne. Not sweat.

But outside.

Like asphalt and adrenaline.

Something happened tonight. I know that weight when it returns, quiet, but buzzing under the surface. Knight doesn't always bleed, but he hums. And when he hums, I listen.

The deeper I get into these sessions, the more tangled everything feels.

Cam is searching for clarity.

Jenx is gripping an illusion.

Navi is hiding in couture.

And me?

I'm sitting here journaling in the dark, trying to make sense of my husband's silences.

As therapists, we call it projection when clients dump unresolved feelings onto others.

But what do we call it when your intuition is screaming... and there's no one to hand it to?

Knight is a fortress.

And I live inside his gates.

But lately, the windows feel too tinted.

That black SUV?

He brushed it off.

Said it was "nothing."

Funny thing is... "nothing" doesn't follow you twice.

And this envelope?

The one I found in my drawer with no fingerprints and silver ink that still smells fresh?

It's sitting next to my tea like it belongs here.

"The more you uncover... the closer it gets."

That's not a warning.

That's a dare.

And I've never been good at walking away from a dare.

Knight thinks he's protecting me.

But what if the real danger isn't outside?

What if it's already slipped through the door with a Hermès bag and a story too polished to be real?

Tomorrow I have Navi at 9:00.

But tonight?

I'm wide awake...

listening to SWV ask for what I thought I already had.

— MH

KNIGHT TIME

Knight & Monroe's Home | DUMBO, Brooklyn
Wednesday | 12:03 a.m.

The air was thick with that post-rain hush. Brooklyn slept hard beneath them, but inside their brownstone, time wasn't moving. Monroe lay still beneath the Egyptian cotton sheets, eyes tracking Knight's every step from the bathroom to the window. He hadn't said much since dinner. Bare chest. Black silk pajama pants hanging low. That vein in his neck pulsing like it was trying to say something his mouth wouldn't.

She waited.

Knight stood by the window, back to her, one hand resting on the pane like it was holding him up. The other clutched a glass of Yamazaki 18. Neat.

He hadn't even sipped it.

"You not gonna talk to me?" she asked softly.

A beat. Then two.

"I was eleven when I watched a man take his last breath," he said, still facing the glass. "Not on TV. Not in a movie. Real life. My uncle. Marcy Projects. Wrong dice game. One second he was talking tough... next second, he was bleeding out on a milk crate."

Monroe sat up slowly, heart in her throat.

Knight turned, the city lights painting one half of his face in gold, the other in shadow. His voice was even. Cold-smooth.

"You know what messed me up the most?" he continued. "Not the blood. Not the way his eyes got wide and still. It was how fast everybody stepped over him. Like his body was just an obstacle in their night."

He finally walked to the bed, slowly. Sat on the edge.

"I promised myself then, nobody I love will ever get stepped over."

Monroe reached for his hand. It was trembling.

"You've never told me that," she whispered.

"There's a lot I've never told you."

He looked at her, those deep-set eyes holding storms and softness.

"I used to be a bad man, Ro. The kind people only say good things about you at the repass. I did things… things that would make you look at me different. But you…"

His voice cracked.

"You made God feel real to me."

She blinked. Hard.

Knight placed the untouched drink on the floor. Climbed into bed. Pulled her against him like he needed her heartbeat to quiet the ones in his memory.

"I don't pray out loud much," he whispered against her ear, "but for you…"

He took her hand. Interlaced their fingers. Closed his eyes.

And then came the prayer.

"God…

Thank you for giving me a woman who sees the good in a man who spent most of his life hiding it. Let my love be her healing, not her hurt.

Let my arms be where she forgets what pain ever felt like.

And if there's ever a day I forget how to love her, take my voice before You take her peace. Amen."

Monroe didn't move.

She couldn't.

Tears slipped sideways across her face, soaking into his chest.

Because this wasn't safety.

This was sanctuary.

And she knew, without a single doubt.

She was loved by a man who had once walked through hell bare-foot...

Just to build heaven for her.

KNIGHT'S FLASHBACK
The Clean Up
Wednesday | 1:07 a.m.

He didn't mean to fall asleep.

But Monroe had that kind of presence.

The kind that slowed your breathing and quieted your demons.

For a while.

Her head was on his chest.

Her leg draped over his.

Her exhale was the only soundtrack.

But Knight's mind?

It had slipped away.

Back.

2009.

Outside a bodega on Clifton Place & Nostrand.

Midnight.

Rain falling sideways.

The first thing he noticed was the scream.

It wasn't loud; it was choked.

Cut short like someone tried to silence it before it finished being scared.

Knight was 23 then.

Malik Woods.

Hoodie soaked.

Timbs pounding pavement.

His hands were still shaking from the fight he'd just left behind three blocks over. Somebody had pulled a knife. Knight left him bleeding and breathless.

He was heading home.

But that scream stopped time.

He ducked behind the bodega.

Gun drawn.

Every instinct firing at once.

She was there.

Pressed against the wall. A girl no older than sixteen.

Her pink bubble coat soaked to the core.

Mouth gagged.

Eyes wide.

The man on her was twice her size,

one hand on her throat,

the other fumbling with his belt.

Knight didn't hesitate.

One shot. Center mass.

The man fell, face-first into the puddle.

The girl didn't run.

She stared at Knight.

Blood on his hoodie.

Rain hitting both of them like a baptism.

She whispered, "Thank you."

Then bolted into the night.

Knight never told a soul.

But he checked the papers every day for a week.

No report.

No girl. No mention of a body.

And for years, the memory haunted him,

not because he pulled the trigger…

But because he didn't know her name.

BACK TO PRESENT DAY

Wide awake, Knight stared at the ceiling.

Monroe stirred. Shifted closer.

He kissed her forehead and whispered a prayer.

Then turned his eyes to the shadows outside their window.

Because earlier that day…

A young woman walked past Monroe's practice.

Pink trench coat.

Hazel eyes.

And the same dimple.

KNIGHT | THE WAY HE MOVES

Somewhere in Clinton Hill, Brooklyn

Thursday | 8:22 AM

Knight didn't walk; he moved like concrete had memory.

Like every sidewalk in Brooklyn owed him something.

He slipped through the city like a story only old heads knew.

No fanfare. No noise. Just presence.

Dark denim. Black hoodie. Everything clean. Crisp.

His black Timbs whispered across the pavement. Laced, not tied. No scuffs.

Brooklyn money. The kind earned, not gifted.

He paused at the corner store on Greene Ave.

Dapped up the owner, nodded to a kid on a bike.

Everybody respected Knight, but nobody knew what he did.

Except that he was the guy you call when it's already too late.

His Range Rover sat waiting, matte black, tinted windows, always facing out.

Control.

Always.

He slid in, adjusted the rearview mirror, and sat for a second.

Then he reached inside the center console.

Pulled out a small velvet box.

Opened it.

Inside:

A platinum ring. Clean lines. Understated. Heavy.

Not for Monroe.

For the past he buried.

For the promise he made the day he walked away from that life.

His phone buzzed.

Unknown number.

He didn't answer.

Knight rolled his neck, like the past was still sitting on it.

He tucked the ring back into the console.

Not because he was hiding it.

Because he never forgets.

Never.

That's why he prays over Monroe every night.

That's why he watches windows before mirrors.

That's why he never lets his phone die,

because protection doesn't clock out.

He looked up.

A black SUV, same as his, pulled slowly down the street.

Same tints. Same rims. Same make.

It stopped.

Didn't park.

Didn't honk.

Just paused.

Knight squinted.

Then the SUV drove off.

No plates on the back.

He didn't chase it.

Didn't flinch.

Just whispered, under his breath.

"I told you once. Don't come near her."

Then he pulled off.

NAVI | UNSCHEDULED VISIT

Dr. Hunter's Office

Friday | 4:15 p.m.

Navi entered the room with her usual presence, curated, composed, and camera-ready. Her Bottega shades concealed hazel eyes that rarely revealed more than she allowed. A Fendi trench coat wrapped tightly around her waist, carrying secrets like fabric.

"Morning," she said. Her voice trembled just enough for Monroe to notice. It was the first time she had walked in without a compliment, a flex, or a line borrowed from her social captions.

Monroe watched her carefully.

"What are we unpacking today, Navi?"

"The truth. Or at least my version of it."

She slipped off her coat and laid it across the chair, revealing a deep purple two-piece set. It was luxurious but soft, vulnerable in a way that caught Monroe's attention.

"I have spent years branding myself as unforgettable," Navi admitted. "The kind of woman you see once and regret losing forever."

Monroe tilted her head.

"That sounds exhausting."

"It is." Navi's voice cracked.

For the first time, she looked almost unrecognizable, stripped of her polish.

"I hate who I have become."

Monroe leaned in gently.

"Tell me why."

"Because I never know if they want me, or the product I've become.

Every day I sell myself with likes, trips, and experiences.

And at night, I cry over a man I knew did not love me.

Because at least I was not alone."

Monroe's throat tightened. "And who was that man?"

"He told me his name was K. Said it stood for Kingdom.

He never gave me a last name."

Monroe's heart stumbled.

"He did not want pictures. He did not want social posts.

But he made me feel covered, safe.

Like if I asked for the moon, he would rent NASA."

Monroe steadied her voice. "And then?"

Navi reached into her Prada clutch and placed a valet ticket on the table.

"This was from our last date. A restaurant in Clinton Hill. He never showed.

But when I arrived, I saw him across the street.

He was holding the hand of a woman with natural curls. He was laughing.

He was protecting her the way he once protected me."

Monroe's chest went tight. Her curls had been pinned up that night.

Knight had taken her to that very restaurant.

Navi's tone grew sharper. "He saw me. He did not flinch.

He only nodded, as if we were strangers living in separate lanes."

"And you never confronted him?" Monroe asked softly.

"How do you confront a ghost?"

The room fell into silence.

Navi's eyes filled.

"I came here to detox from men.

I did not expect to mourn someone still alive."

Monroe rose slowly and crossed the room.

She took Navi's hand and held it firmly.

"Grief wears many faces.

Sometimes we grieve the hope we had for someone.

Sometimes we grieve the parts of ourselves we gave away for love."

Tears streamed freely down Navi's face.

"I think he was protecting me from himself.

I think I loved a man who was built for someone else."

Monroe's voice steadied. "That does not make your love less real."

"So what do I do now?"

"Now you stop performing. You learn who you are without the luxury.

Without the camera. Without the man.

Because you, Navi Blu, are still worth choosing."

Navi collapsed into Monroe's arms.

Makeup smudged, posture forgotten, she sobbed like a woman finally letting go of a diamond she had choked on for too long.

Outside, an SUV rolled past. Its shape was eerie, familiar.

It looked just like Knight's.

Monroe kept her face composed, but her spirit stirred.

KNIGHT | TWELVE YEARS CHOSEN

Friday | 6:32 p.m.

The entryway had never looked like this before.

The air carried the weight of roses, rich and full, their scent rising like lit incense. Red roses filled every corner, not scattered, not rushed, but placed with intention.

Twelve dozen in bloom. Each vase stood like an altar, each petal a vow.

It was not flowers Monroe was walking into. It was a testimony.

Twelve years. Twelve dozen.

Twelve times over, he had chosen her.

The key had turned like always, but Monroe knew something was different the moment she stepped inside. Before she could even set her purse down, love had already found her at the door. The entryway. The living room. The kitchen.

Even one waiting on the fridge.

On the marble island sat a chilled bottle of prosecco, two flutes,

and a note in Knight's sharp handwriting.

Just because.

You are not just the best part of my life.

You are my life.

– K.

Soft music drifted from the Bluetooth speaker near the staircase.

Eric Benét and Tamia, *Spend My Life with You*. Smooth.

Timeless. Exactly like Knight.

Monroe blinked against tears she had not realized had formed.

Then she heard him. Footsteps. Slow. Deliberate.

Knight stepped in from the patio. A plain black tee, sweats, barefoot.

Nothing staged. Just him. Smiling like he already knew how she would react.

She lost her breath. Not to drama or tears,

but to the way peace can take the air from your lungs

when it finally shows up and stays.

Knight had never needed big speeches.

He turned moments into monuments without saying a word.

He pulled her close. Strong arms. Warm chest.

Familiar scent. Oud for Greatness mixing with the air, thick with jasmine and Jo Malone.

He held her like a vow.

"Twelve years ago, I did not know what peace felt like," he whispered against her ear. "Now it sleeps next to me, prays for me, and looks like you."

Monroe's breath caught.

He kissed her forehead. Then her temple. Then her lips. Soft. Slow. No audience. No cameras. Just the kind of love that felt rare and holy.

She reached for her phone and switched the playlist. Musiq Soulchild's "Love". The room shifted. Sacred. Intimate. She sang softly, "So many people use your name in vain…"

Knight bent close, kissed her forehead again, and whispered, "But never me. Never with you."

He took her by the hand and led her to the middle of the floor. Placed her arms around his neck while he bent down, embracing her close, and started slow dancing.

"You give the world your mind every day, Halo," he said quietly.

"I just wanted to remind you that you already have mine."

Monroe wept. She did not analyze.

She did not question. She only received.

Later, they danced in the kitchen with no music but their own. Her feet rested on top of his untied Timbs. She liked to seem like she was taller.

This was what safety looked like when it dressed itself in peace.

This was love, twelve years chosen.

MONROE'S JOURNAL

Friday | 10:41 p.m.

Playlist: "Love" by Musiq Soulchild

CLIENT | Navi | Unscheduled Visit

There were roses in the foyer.

Twelve dozen.

Red. Full bloom.

Lush like they were breathing.

One dozen for every year we've been together.

And he placed them at the door, my door, so I couldn't miss the message.

Before I could even step into the house, love had already greeted me.

There was more.

The living room.

The kitchen.

Even one in the fridge.

Knight has never needed big speeches.

He's the kind of man who turns moments into monuments, without saying a word.

And when I finally found him... barefoot in the hallway, in sweats and a plain black tee, smiling like he already knew how I'd react, I lost it.

Not the tears. Not the drama. Just... breath. Gone.

Because this is what safety feels like when it's dressed in peace.

When love shows up like routine.

When the house smells like Jo Malone and jasmine, and the man in front of you is both home and hope.

He didn't say, "You're my everything."

He said, "I got you."

And meant it.

We danced. No music.

Just kitchen tile, my bare feet on top of his Timbs,

and the kind of silence that claps back at loneliness.

I played Musiq Soulchild's *"Love."*

It felt right.

It felt holy.

And when I sang along softly.

"So many people use your name in vain..."

Knight leaned down, kissed my forehead, and whispered,

"But never me. Never with you."

God, I don't know what I did to deserve this man.

But thank you for making him from the things I didn't even know how to pray for.

Because I've healed hearts...

But he healed mine.

— MH

CAM | SESSION FIVE

Dr. Hunter's Office

Saturday | 9:00 AM

Cam walked in dressed like a decision, not a disguise.

Oversized black hoodie pulled tight. Black fitted jeans hugging sharp lines. Gold hoops catching the dim light, and fresh black Timbs tied the way Brooklyn men tie respect into their stride.

She didn't wait for Monroe to greet her. She sat forward, elbows on her knees, eyes locked. "I need truth," she said, her tone flat but quivering beneath.

Monroe closed her notebook slowly, palms folding like she was about to pray.

"Then ask the question you've been avoiding."

Cam's jaw flexed.

"Am I worthy of peace... or just survival?"

Silence pressed the room like humidity.

Monroe leaned in, her voice velvet sharpened with steel.

"Cam, the hood taught you checkers. Quick moves. Jump or get jumped. Don't think, react. That game keeps you alive, but it never lets you win.

What you're asking me? That's not a checkers question. That's chess."

Cam blinked.

"In checkers," Monroe continued, "you become a king by surviving to the other side. But in chess? The Queen starts powerful. The Queen doesn't wait for permission to move. She doesn't need to cross the board to earn worth. She already has it."

Cam's breath shook.

"Then why do I keep attracting men who treat me like a pawn?"

Monroe's eyes narrowed.

"Because you've been sitting at their tables. Men who still think love is checkers. Fast moves, shortcuts, no strategy. They don't know how to see a Queen, so they reduce her to a piece they can sacrifice."

Cam's voice cracked.

"So what do I do? Flip the board?"

Monroe's tone sliced through the room.

"No. You change the game entirely. You stop auditioning for men who love chaos and you start demanding men who can sit in peace without flinching.

Because Queens don't just play to survive.

Queens protect the kingdom."

Tears slid down Cam's cheeks, but she didn't fold.

"I want to be chosen for my peace."

"Again," Monroe said, firmer.

Cam's voice rose. "I want to be chosen for my peace!"

Her hands balled into fists, her Timbs planted like anchors.

Monroe softened, but didn't let her off the hook.

"Say it like a move, not a wish."

Cam leaned forward, eyes sharp.

"If you can't choose me for my peace, you don't get me at all."

The air crackled.

Monroe's heart ached at the weight of it. She pointed at Cam's boots.

"Nineteen years old, a man in black Timbs pulled you out of chaos. That's the moment you learned what protection could feel like.

But protection is not peace.

It's the beginning, not the ending.

You've been waiting for him to show up again, when the truth is," she leaned in, whisper-precise, "you laced those boots yourself today. You're the protection now."

Cam exhaled like a storm breaking.

"All black like the omen," she whispered. "But this time... I'm the prophecy."

MONROE'S JOURNAL

DUMBO Loft

Saturday | 11:45 p.m.

CLIENT | Cam | Session Five

Cam said it clean today: "I want to be chosen for my peace."

Not strength. Not survival. Peace. That's the first time she's stopped performing for applause and started auditioning for silence.

She walked into my office, laced in black Timbs, the same boots that once pulled her out of chaos. Only this time, she didn't wait for Knightmare. She declared herself the prophecy.

But the streets won't let her rest.

I think about how Bed-Stuy used to feel. Block parties on Greene Ave, GS 3s lining curbs, dice games running hot. Now it's green juice bars and yoga studios. Gentrification painted over the corners, but the ghosts remain. Cam carries them in her chest.

The SUV is circling all of us, Navi, Jenx, and Cam. Maybe it's circling me most of all.

I told Cam Queens don't just play the board, they flip it. But tonight, I wonder if I'm telling myself the same thing. Because the Queen is the most dangerous piece. But she's also the most hunted.

And if this game has brought us all together, then it's not just Bed-Stuy that's in play.

It's me.

— MH

CAM | OUTSIDE
Quincy & Bedford | Bed-Stuy

Saturday | Midnight

Fog coiled low over Bedford Avenue, swallowing corners, bending halos around flickering streetlights. The block smelled like fried chicken grease, incense smoke, and rain still sweating out of the bricks.

Cam parked a block away and walked toward Quincy & Bedford, where the Biggie mural rose three stories tall. His crowned head glowed under the lamp like a stained-glass window, watching his borough. Spread love, it's the Brooklyn way, scrawled in tags nearby, faded but un-erasable.

She came cloaked in shadow: black hoodie pulled up, black jeans, gold hoops gleaming, fresh black Timbs striking the sidewalk with authority.

"All black like the omen," she muttered. Lil' Kim's line floating out like a mantra.

But the block wasn't the block she grew up with. The old bodega on the corner was now a cold-pressed juice spot. The barber shop next to it had become a boutique selling plants in mason jars. A bike-share rack lined the curb where dice games once ran until cops raided. Bed-Stuy had been repainted, but the bones still whispered.

Her phone buzzed.

BRING WHAT'S HIS. COME ALONE.

Her hand gripped the spare fob in her pocket, steel biting through fabric. Across from Biggie's face, the matte black SUV idled, engine low, headlights dead. It didn't just sit. It waited.

Cam stopped beneath Biggie's crown, heart pounding, fog pressing close.

She whispered to herself, "Queens don't wait to be crowned. Queens flip the board!"

Through the SUV's cracked window, faint music spilled out, Mary J. Blige, *"I can't be without you, babe..."* The hook floated like a taunt, like an old wound replayed.

Cam's throat tightened, but she straightened, hoodie casting a shadow. "I can," she said aloud, her words bouncing off the mural like testimony.

She stepped forward once. Timbs hit the wet concrete, the sound loud, deliberate. Echoing Knight, mirroring the man who once shielded her, but this time, no savior in sight.

Just Cam.

Not a pawn. Not a performer.

A Queen, standing under the King's crown, making her own move.

PILLOW TALK
Sunday | 12:12 a.m.

The bedroom was dark except for the thin glow of the hallway light leaking through the cracked door. Shadows stretched across the walls, long and restless. Monroe lay on her side, back to Knight, her eyes wide, counting the rhythm of his breaths like clock ticks.

The mattress dipped as he shifted, one leg sliding under the covers. His presence pressed into the room, heavy as gravity, impossible to ignore.

"You sleep?" His voice slipped into the quiet, roughened by fatigue.

She let the question hang before answering. "Almost."

"You was quiet when I got in."

"Long day."

"What, them therapy sessions wearing you out?"

His words carried playfulness, but the edge beneath settled in her chest like a stone.

Monroe let out a thin laugh. "Something like that."

He leaned in, his chest radiating heat against her back, his arm curving over her waist with the certainty of muscle memory. The gesture was tender, familiar, but it carried a weight tonight she could not shake.

"You good, Halo?"

Her eyes opened at the name. Halo. A word that belonged only to him, spoken softly but binding, a crown and a chain all at once.

"Yeah. Just thinking."

"What about?"

She turned to face him. His eyes were half-lidded, calm, drifting toward sleep. But she searched them anyway, hunting for the part he did not show.

"Have you ever had to save someone's life?"

The air between them thickened. He did not move. He did not blink. The silence was not empty. It was alive, coiled, waiting. Five seconds. Ten. Her pulse climbed until it roared in her ears.

"Yeah."

Her voice pushed through the heaviness. "More than once?"

Another pause. Shorter, but sharper. His gaze stayed locked, unblinking, as if deciding how much she could bear.

"Yeah. More than once."

He kissed her forehead then, the motion tender, almost rehearsed, before pulling her against his chest and tucking her beneath his chin the way he always did. To anyone else, it would have looked like love. To Monroe, it felt like a cover.

She stayed awake, tracing slow patterns on his shoulder with her fingertips. Each circle carried a question. Each line carried a silent prayer for truth. The night stretched long, and in the quiet she thought she heard something slip between the beats of his heart.

Not a word, but a weight. Not a sound, but the shape of a memory too heavy to bury. It pressed into her skin like a secret, and for the first time, she wondered if the lives he saved were the same that chained him now.

JENX | SESSION FIVE

Dr. Hunter's Office

Monday | 7:03 a.m.

Jenx came in like the storm before the rain.

Hood half-up. Olive utility jacket open. Black tank. Cargo pants tucked into black Timbs scuffed just right, not fashion, but memory. Around her neck swung a thin chain with a flash drive instead of a charm. Jenx wore leverage like jewelry.

She didn't sit immediately. She prowled. Stood by the bookshelf, scanning the spines like they were mugshots. Finally dropped into the velvet chair, body folding like a weight had been welded onto her shoulders.

"You ever notice," she began, voice low but sharp, "the hood teaches you to love like a lookout? One eye on the kiss, one eye on the corner."

Monroe tilted her head. "Vigilance became intimacy. You've confused paranoia with passion."

Jenx smirked, bitter. "Banks called it loyalty. I called it oxygen. Now I know it was just overtime." She tapped the flash drive. "Insurance. Ledgers that keep men breathing, or get them buried."

"What does holding it do for you?" Monroe asked softly, but her tone pressed.

"Keeps me from forgetting I kept him alive."

Monroe leaned in, elbows on her knees. Her voice turned scalpel.

"Say your fear."

Jenx looked down, thumb sliding across the drive like it was a rosary. "If I stop protecting him, I have to protect myself. And I don't know if I can."

"Correction," Monroe said, eyes steady. "You don't know if you're allowed to.

The block crowned you for endurance, not ease. Loyalty without reciprocity isn't love, it's labor. You're not betraying Banks by leaving. You're resigning from unpaid work."

Her jaw flexed. "And if the hood calls me disloyal?"

"Then let them play checkers while you learn chess," Monroe replied. "Checkers-loyalty stays until it's crowned. Chess-loyalty remembers the Queen ends the game."

The crack showed, barely, in Jenx's eyes.

Monroe pushed deeper. "Say it. Out loud. I am more than his ledger."

Jenx hesitated. "I am more than his ledger."

"Again," Monroe pressed.

This time, stronger: "I am more than his ledger."

Monroe nodded once. "Good. Because survival was your initiation. But thriving? That's your birthright. Queens don't just guard kings. Queens move in ways kings never can."

Jenx slid the drive into her pocket like a weapon, chain clinking softly. "Then it's my move."

And under her breath, she hummed the lyrics she'd been looping all week from Courtney Berry's "Incredible".

You can do anything you put your mind to.

You're a star.

You're a diamond.

You're a masterpiece.

You don't have to hide.

MONROE'S JOURNAL

Monday | 10:24 a.m.

CLIENT | Jenx | Session Five

Jenx wore leverage like legacy. A flash drive where a cross might hang. She thought leaving Banks was betrayal. But betrayal is a leash word men use to keep women small. Freedom is heavier because it demands you carry yourself.

We dismantled her nervous system today. Took apart the wiring that said vigilance is love and loyalty is oxygen. I told her what nobody in her world ever has: Loyalty without reciprocity isn't love, it's labor. She inhaled that like air for the first time.

Then she said it, out loud, what I needed her to believe: I am more than his ledger.

Her body shook when she spoke it, like the sentence unlocked a memory. Maybe that's what healing really is, replacing survival mantras with living ones.

She's walked out of my office with receipts that can burn the borough. The SUVs are multiplying. The texts have synchronized. My own phone buzzed again: MOVE.

That's not advice. That's a dare.

I keep thinking of the board. Checkers is fast wounds. Chess is long wars. Checkers crowns you only after you bleed across the squares. Chess remembers: Queens move the farthest. Queens end the game. Which is why Queens are hunted first.

And Jenx, whether the block crowns her or not, is still standing. Still singing. Still incredible.

If the hood wants to rename her disloyal, so be it. History will rename her legendary.

— MH

JENX | OUTSIDE

Myrtle–Broadway | J/M/Z Train

Monday | 11:04 p.m.

The tracks above screamed their iron lullaby; the air was painted rust by lamps.

Jenx stood under the chipped crown mural near the station, hood up, one hand fisting the burner, the other palming the flash drive like it pulsed.

Her headphones playing, *"Incredible"* by Courtney Berry.

Lyrics threading through her bloodstream:

"You're incredible. More beautiful than you know." She mouthed the lyrics.

Not performance. Survival.

The block around her had been gutted and dressed in someone else's clothes.

The dice stoop scrubbed into a smoothie bar.

The bodega that once blasted Beenie Man now sold oat milk and matcha. Old heads vanished. New faces dog-walked designer doodles where pit bulls used to stand guard.

"Bed-Stuy turned Brooklyn-lite," she muttered. "Ghosts without rent control."

Her phone buzzed.

TRADE. LEDGER FOR A NAME

COME ALONE. DON'T BE LATE.

Pin: Fort Greene Park 12:30am.

Across the service road, the matte black SUV idled beneath a dead streetlight.

Engine low.

Jenx smirked, wiping her thumb across the flash drive.

"You ain't the only one with receipts."

She pushed off the mural. Timbs pounding concrete, echoes of the man she once described. The SUV didn't move, just watched.

As she crossed Myrtle, *"Incredible"* played softly in her ears.

She said it aloud this time, like gospel meant only for her.

The words tasted dangerous.

The kind of danger that saves.

NAVI | SESSION FIVE

Dr. Hunter's Office

Wednesday | 8:08 AM

Navi didn't arrive like royalty this time. She arrived like a confession.

No platinum waves. No lashes. No diamond bag. Just her.

Hair braided back, edges unstyled. Oversized cream cashmere sweater, black leggings, and silver Nike P-6000. She looked... reachable. And that made her more untouchable than ever.

She sat down slowly, eyes scanning the candleless room. Jo Malone was absent. Only the smell of rain off the East River.

"Doc..." she started, voice cracked raw. "I don't think I know how to exist without performing."

Monroe leaned forward, tone surgical. "Performing is checkers. It looks quick, loud, obvious. Living is chess. It's patient, strategic, silent. Which board have you been playing on?"

Navi exhaled, half-laugh, half-choke. "I been teaching the world how to clap while I die inside. The Hood Princess. The one everybody wanted to watch. You ever realized crowns can choke?"

"You told me in session one that nobody carries Monique," Monroe reminded her. "Say it now. Who carries you?"

Her eyes glistened. "Nobody. But God. I guess."

Monroe let the silence sit. Then softly, "Even God moves through people. If you don't let anyone carry you, you've mistaken survival for worship."

That cracked her. She looked down, tears falling like diamonds unfastened.

She whispered, almost a hymn, "Today I wear a smile, because I'm no longer where I was…"

Monroe recognized it, Jules Juda's "Movement." Navi wasn't quoting Instagram this time. She was quoting survival.

Monroe pressed. "That smile is not the product. It's the prophecy. Movement doesn't mean speed. It means transformation. And transformation requires surrender."

Navi shook her head. "I don't know who I am without the Birkin. Without the men. Without the shine."

"Correction," Monroe said sharply. "You don't know who you are yet. But the Birkin was checkers. Monique? She's the Queen. And Queens don't need permission to end games."

Silence. Monroe's thoughts flashed back to the Birkin in the video.

Navi nodded once. Slow. Final.

MONROE'S JOURNAL

Wednesday | 11:04 a.m.

CLIENT | Navi | Session Five

Navi walked in today stripped of her costume. No unit. No lashes. No throne. Just Monique. And in that moment, I saw something luxury could never counterfeit, fragility as power.

She said nobody carries her. That's not strength. That's starvation. The world has clapped so long for her performance that she's forgotten applause is not affection.

I told her survival was checkers. Chess is different. Chess is patience. Chess is sacrifice. Chess is legacy. Queens end games, but only if they survive long enough to see the board.

And here's the part that chills me: each of them, Cam, Jenx, and Navi, is being circled by the same SUV. Same shadow. Same watcher. Different corners.

My phone buzzed again tonight. Same message. MOVE.

The more I connect their stories, the clearer it becomes: this isn't coincidence. This is choreography. They've been placed on my board.

And Queens?

Queens are always the first piece hunted.

— MH

NAVI | OUTSIDE

Madison Avenue Penthouse

Wednesday | 10:31 p.m.

The marble floor was warm beneath her feet, but the chill in her chest refused to leave.

She had turned the heat on the moment she entered, a ritual of comfort, a way to make the penthouse feel less like a museum and more like a home. Marble, orchids, mirrors. The perfection pressed in around her. Barefoot, sweater slipping off one shoulder, she crossed the room with a glass of red wine she didn't intend to drink.

On the counter sat the burner phone.

One missed call.

No number.

No voicemail.

Silence that weighed heavier than sound.

She opened her laptop. Not Instagram. Not her brand reports. Not the glossy facade she fed to strangers. Tonight, she opened the encrypted folder. The one that held the names. The secrets. The files she collected were like weapons.

Then it happened.

A sharp tap on marble.

Her head snapped up. The sound of something small and solid rolling across the counter broke her concentration clean in two.

She turned.

The pawn sat there. Black. Heavy. Its slow spin on the countertop proved it had just been placed.

Her pulse hammered.

She reached for it, thumb grazing its surface. The base shifted loose. Inside, folded tight, a strip of photo paper.

She unfolded it with shaking hands.

Her own face stared back. Caught mid-stride, crossing Madison Avenue. Barefoot. Tonight.

Her stomach dropped. Whoever was playing this game wasn't just inside her home. They were outside too. Watching. Recording.

The burner phone lit again. Same call. No number. This time, it buzzed against the marble like it was alive.

She moved toward the terrace, glass in hand, every muscle trembling, though the floor burned warm beneath her feet.

Beyond the orchids and mirrored glass, the matte black SUV had moved closer. Engine alive. Lights off. Waiting.

She whispered into the stillness, forcing the words out.

"I am not the pawn."

But the photo in her hand said otherwise.

The game had crossed her threshold.

And Navi Blu was no longer watching it unfold.

She was inside it.

PILLOW TALK
Wednesday | 12:21 a.m.

The bedroom was dark except for the thin glow of the hallway light peeking through the cracked door. Shadows stretched across the walls, long and restless. Monroe lay on her side, back to Knight, her eyes wide, counting the rhythm of his breaths like clock ticks.

The mattress dipped as he shifted, one leg sliding under the covers. His presence pressed into the room, heavy as gravity, impossible to ignore.

"You sleep?" His voice slipped into the quiet, roughened by fatigue.

She let the question hang before answering. "Almost."

"You was quiet when I got in."

"Long day."

"What, them therapy sessions wearing you out?" His words carried playfulness, but underneath was an edge that settled in her chest like a stone.

Monroe let out a thin laugh. "Something like that."

He leaned in, his chest radiating heat against her back, his arm curving over her waist with the certainty of muscle memory. The gesture was tender, familiar, but it carried a weight tonight she could not shake.

"You good, Halo?"

Her eyes opened at the name. Halo. A word that belonged only to him, spoken softly but binding, a crown and a chain all at once.

"Yeah. Just thinking."

"What about?"

She turned to face him. His eyes were half-lidded, calm, drifting toward sleep. But she searched them anyway, hunting for the part he did not show.

"Have you ever had to save someone's life?"

The air between them thickened. He did not move. He did not blink. The silence was not empty. It was alive, coiled, waiting. Five seconds. Ten. Her pulse climbed until it roared in her ears.

"Yeah."

Her voice pushed through the heaviness. "More than once?"

Another pause. Shorter, but sharper. His gaze stayed locked, unblinking, as if deciding how much she could bear.

"Yeah. More than once."

He kissed her forehead then, the motion tender, almost rehearsed, before pulling her against his chest and tucking her beneath his chin the way he always did. To anyone else, it would have looked like love. To Monroe, it felt like a cover.

She stayed awake, tracing slow patterns on his shoulder with her fingertips. Each circle carried a question. Each line carried a silent prayer for truth. The night stretched long, and in the quiet she thought she heard something slip between the beats of his heart.

Not a word, but a weight. Not a sound, but the shape of a memory too heavy to bury. It pressed into her skin like a secret, and for the first time, she wondered if the lives he saved were the same that chained him now.

BREADCRUMB

Monroe's Office | Top Floor

Thursday | 6:27 p.m.

The elevator doors opened slowly.

Too slow.

Monroe stepped out, umbrella dripping, heart pounding under calm breath.

The hallway smelled like lavender and Lysol, normal.

Everything was too normal.

And that's what made it feel… wrong.

She reached her office door.

Unlocked.

That wasn't possible.

She always locked it. Twice.

It was muscle memory.

She opened it, one inch at a time.

Nothing was out of place.

Not the orchids by the window.

Not the Jo Malone candle, still unlit.

Not even the coffee cup with her lipstick print from this morning.

But the air was different.

Warmer.

Thicker.

Like someone had just exhaled and left it behind.

She stepped inside.

The door clicked shut behind her.

She dropped her keys into the bowl.

Then she saw it.

A second envelope.

This one wasn't on her desk.

It was taped, neatly, to her full-length mirror.

Another black envelope.

Same silver ink.

But this time… the words?

"You're not the only one watching."

Monroe stared at her reflection.

She looked composed.

But she didn't feel it.

She peeled the envelope off the mirror with surgical control and opened it with a letter opener from her desk.

Inside:

A Polaroid.

Of her.

From behind.

Standing in her office.

Hair up. White blouse. Writing in her journal.

Yesterday.

Her breath caught.

She checked the camera.

Still green. Still live.

No tampering.

Someone had been inside.

Someone who knew her angle.

Her routines.

Her wardrobe.

She clutched the envelope, pulled out her phone, and dialed Knight.

One ring. Two. Three.

Voicemail.

She hung up.

Typed:

Where were you at 3:14 yesterday?

No reply.

She turned the lights off.

Sat in her desk chair.

And for the first time in years…

Monroe Hunter felt hunted.

THE KEY TO EVERYTHING

Saturday | 11:15 a.m.

It was supposed to be a regular Saturday.

Just paperwork and maybe a solo glass of wine at home.

But as Monroe stepped out of her home, the air shifted.

A black Rolls-Royce Cullinan idled at the curb.

Engine humming low. The kind of hum that vibrated through her chest.

A uniformed driver stepped out, handed her a single black envelope.

Thick. Matte. Warm like it had been clutched for hours.

The note inside, handwritten in Knight's ink:

I can't wait to see you, Halo.

I know we have to talk.

But tonight... I promise, you'll know it all.

She didn't ask questions.

Not yet.

Inside the Cullinan, the scent of pink garden roses overwhelmed her.

Her color. Her softness.

A bouquet beside her seat.

The red carpet was rolled out when she arrived at The Chart House in Weehawken. Private entrance. Skyline view.

The room?

Roses.

One thousand two hundred red long-stems lined the walls, filled the ceiling's perimeter, and bloomed from the table's centerpiece. One hundred roses for every year they'd been together.

Knight stood there.

Dressed in a crisp obsidian suit. Shirt unbuttoned at the collar.

Vulnerability in his posture. A soft fire in his eyes.

He didn't speak.

Just handed her a small, locked black velvet box,

a golden latch glinting beneath candlelight.

Tied to it,

After I tell you everything...

If you open this, you'll find the key to our new beginning.

If not, I'll understand.

She held it like it was alive.

They sat.

And for the next forty-two minutes, Knight unraveled a story that bent time.

He told her about the Norgate Crew.

How he walked away after Simone, his ex-girlfriend, disappeared with federal protection.

How his twin brother Sire stayed in the life, wearing Knight's face and ruining his name.

How he found Simone again... and buried the truth to protect Monroe from her.

Then. Something darker.

"The women you've been coaching..." he said.

"They weren't coincidences."

Monroe's throat almost closed.

"Cam's father used to run with my uncle," he continued.

"They were tight. One day, she was in the midst of a shootout, and I saved her life.

Jenx is the sister of a guy I grew up with.

Navi… she wasn't just some luxury queen. She was in that house on Madison

because I put her there. For protection."

Monroe blinked.

"And the receptionist at your practice was a former FBI Agent.

I had her there to provide safety and inform me of any mishaps

I would have to get in front of."

The puzzle slammed together.

"You sent them to me…"

"To fix what I broke," he confessed.

The air cracked.

Monroe couldn't find her voice.

"You weren't just my safe space," Knight said.

"You were my redemption. And I knew if I didn't tell you…

I'd lose the only good thing that ever came from all of this."

Her hand shook as she touched the box again.

"I can't un-live what I've lived," he said softly.

"But if you still believe in me, even now… that box will tell me everything."

He stood up and walked to the window.

Facing the city.

Facing himself.

Monroe sat alone.

Eyes on the latch.

The last line of the note whispered back:

This is your choice now, Halo.

But know this, everything I did, I did for you.

Monroe's mind began to race.

Do I follow my heart or my brain?
Do I open it?
Or do I walk away?

THE SUMMONS

Sunday | 8:28 a.m.

The messages came without warning.

Cam.

Jenx.

Navi.

Banks.

Each received a video.

The screen lit up with an image of themselves, caught exactly where they were at that very moment.

Cam saw her own living room behind her.

Jenx recognized her street corner.

Navi was shown inside her penthouse, the glow of her laptop burning on the table. Banks watched himself sitting in his car, the camera angle impossible, the timing undeniable.

The clips ended abruptly, replaced by a single text.

00:00. 277 Eldert Street. Brooklyn.

By midnight, they each arrived on the block.

The air was still, carrying a heaviness that felt staged.

At the center stood a church with steady brick walls and a weathered sign that read *Mt. Olive Church.*

Banks froze.

He remembered laughter in the yard, folding chairs, suppers in the basement dining hall. The memories pressed at him, equal parts comfort and unease.

At the gate on the side of the church stood a young woman with locs and a beautiful smile. Her presence was soft yet commanding.

In a tone that felt like warm body butter on skin, she said, "Right this way."

Her name was Jazz.

She guided them through the side door and into the dining hall.

The air smelled faintly of wood polish and candle wax.

Folding chairs framed the long tables.

The silence pressed in heavy.

Jazz motioned for them to sit.

From the shadows, a figure emerged.

The receptionist.

For weeks, she had been the polite face behind Monroe's desk, her voice clipped and professional.

But now when she spoke, the sound was different.

Lower.

Stripped of sweetness.

Carrying the weight of truth.

She was Knight's plant, placed carefully to protect Monroe before Monroe ever realized she was in danger.

"It had to be done this way," she said, her tone cutting through the quiet. "You would not have come if you knew what was waiting. Sometimes protection works best when you do not realize you are being protected."

Her eyes locked on each of them in turn.

"Cam... you fight for control, but your heart still bends where it should not."

"Jenx... loyalty keeps you chained, even when the chain is choking you."

"Navi... you shine in the spotlight, but in the dark you cannot bear your own reflection."

"Banks... you have buried too much, but the ground remembers."

The words fell like pieces moved on a board.

They shifted in their seats.

The receptionist was no longer the woman they thought they knew.

She carried Knight's authority in her stance and in her voice.

She leaned forward.

"Checkers is about quick moves.

This is chess.

Every silence, every step, every piece on this board has already been placed.

Tonight is your move."

Banks's jaw tightened.

The mention of chess pulled at him.

He felt Knight's hand in this, a design larger than the moment.

A game that had been unfolding long before he recognized it.

The receptionist let the silence stretch.

Then her voice dropped.

"Where you are going cannot be found by directions alone.

You must be blindfolded.

Not to humiliate you.

Not to frighten you.

But because some places are only revealed when trust is tested.

When the blindfolds come off, you will understand why it had to be this way."

Jazz stepped forward again, her warmth smoothing the sharpness of the moment.

"This way," she said softly.

She escorted them back outside, guiding them toward the black sprinter waiting at the curb. Its engine rumbled low, steady, patient, like the drumbeat of the night.

The night had only just begun.

THE BRIDGE

Sunday | 2:07 p.m.

Monroe's receptionist entered, slipping a tablet into each set of waiting hands.

Screens blinked awake, faces lit with a cold blue glow.

First Came The Proof

Cam's hustles and heartbreaks mapped out like coordinates.

Jenx's coded drops and the condo no one knew about.

Navi's trail of luxury receipts stacked higher than a Brooklyn brownstone.

Banks' moves, clocked down to silence and timing.

Each screen, a mirror.

Each screen, a truth no one thought could be traced.

Then the footage shifted.

The black SUV idling too long outside Monroe's office.

The envelopes with no return address, heavy with intention.

The pawn left behind in Jenx's condo, standing bold against blush walls where no one should have been.

And the words, bold letters scrawled like a warning, burning like a brand.

Behind It All

The words dissolved.

And Simone's face appeared. Wide eyes. Breath caught.

The look of someone just realizing she was being watched.

The semi-circle leaned forward, each reaction its own storm.

Cam's lips parted, a whisper sliding out, raw with disbelief.

Jenx's fingers tapped fast against the edge of the tablet, her body locked still.

Navi's hazel eyes narrowed, studying angles, already calculating.

Banks didn't move at all, his stare cold, heavy, unreadable.

Knight stepped forward into the center.

His presence was steady, unshaken.

His voice cut through the silence like a blade.

"You see it now. I know each of you.

I know your plays, your secrets, your shadows.

And I know the trail that's been haunting all of us. The SUV. The envelopes. The pawn in the condo. The word that burned itself into memory."

He paused, letting Simone's face burn across every screen.

"And this is who it leads to."

The weight of his words settled heavily.

The air tightened.

The semi-circle that had come in scattered now shifted, pulling closer, like pieces finally moved into formation.

Knight's eyes cut through the dark, his voice lower now, Brooklyn thick in his cadence.

"This ain't theory.

This ain't chance.

This is Brooklyn work.

We don't miss.

We don't fold.

And when the board tilts, we set it straight."

He let the words ride, Simone's frozen image glowing back at them.

"In the words of the 50th Law:

Your fears are a kind of prison that confines you within a limited range of action."

The less you fear, the more power you will have and the more fully you will live.

The silence didn't break. It tightened.

Respect and shock braided together in the air.

Knight's gaze swept the room, hard and certain.

"This is where fear ends. And power begins."

THE CLEARPORT

Monday | 12:12 p.m.

The SUVs rolled through the private terminal gate like they owned the asphalt.

Security didn't stop them.

No clipboard raised. No questions asked.

Silence spoke louder than paperwork.

The jet sat at the far end of the tarmac, its nose tilted, cabin lights glowing faintly as if it had been waiting all night.

Doors opened.

They stepped out in formation.

Black Timbs.

Black-on-Black *God Is From Brooklyn* hoodies.

Flight jackets zipped tight.

Not random.

Not scattered.

Synchronized.

Stealth.

Clocked.

Knight walked point, hood shadowing his face, hands loose at his sides like his only weapon was time.

Banks followed half a step behind, flight jacket zipped, shoulders wide enough to block a lane.

Cam peeled left, eyes scanning for exits, every move squared.

Jenx fell into rhythm, hood low, gum quiet, her silence heavier than words.

Navi glided with precision, perfume clinging like smoke and saffron, Baccarat Rouge 540's metallic sweetness staining the cold.

The receptionist trailed close to Knight, eyes on corners, fire escapes, reflections.

Simone stumbled between them, wrists locked tight in Cam's grip, body jerking like she thought she still had choices.

Her heels scraped against the marble of the terminal floor.

"You set me up!" she roared, voice breaking. "Who flipped my line?"

Knight didn't break stride. "Brooklyn."

Simone shook her head, panic ripping through her. "No, no, he would never."

Banks glanced over his shoulder, one look that ended her sentence.

Jenx pressed a gloved hand between Simone's shoulder blades, pushing her forward. Cam yanked her wrist harder, as if stamping the truth into her bones.

Navi took her purse, rifled it open, pulled the burner phone, and dropped it on the tarmac. Her Timbs cracked it into silence.

The jet steps hissed open.

The cabin door swung wide.

The crew moved her up, no words wasted.

Banks lifted her like cargo, legs kicking.

Jenx clamped her mouth shut.

Cam locked her wrists.

Navi moved like smoke.

The receptionist scanned behind them, making sure Brooklyn saw but didn't interfere.

Knight stepped on board last.

The cabin swallowed them whole.

Engines rumbled.

Wheels cut across concrete.

Brooklyn clocked the move, then turned its head, like a borough that already knew the outcome.

* * * * *

The Flight

Inside was leather and silence.

No chatter. No jokes. Just pressure.

Cam sat across from Simone, wrist still in her grip.

Simone tugged, but Cam's hand didn't move, iron disguised as flesh.

Jenx leaned against the wall, hood shadowing her face.

Navi crossed her legs, perfume thick in the cabin, saffron and cedar riding the recycled air like smoke that refused to clear.

Banks posted by the aisle, arms folded, body language saying he could end the flight in one move if he wanted.

The receptionist stood by the door, steady, chin lifted, eyes cataloguing every twitch Simone made.

Knight sat dead center, hood up, still as a monument.

Simone broke first.

"This is illegal! You can't."

Banks cut in. "Words."

Her chest rattled. "Why me? What did I do?"

Knight finally lifted his head, voice deep, Brooklyn carved into every syllable.

"You touched Halo."

Simone's lips trembled. "I was protecting her."

Jenx laughed, one sharp sound that felt like a slap.

"That's what you call stalking?"

Navi leaned forward, voice smooth, deadly.

"Queens don't need pawns pretending to guard them."

The engines surged, pressing Simone's back into leather.

She realized then that nobody alive even knew she was in the sky.

BRANDED

Tuesday | 8:25 a.m.

Concrete. No windows. No clocks. Just a chair bolted center, steel cuffs waiting.

They dragged Simone into place. Cam slammed her wrists into the restraints, steel clanking shut. Banks locked her ankles, no struggle needed. Jenx shoved her down hard enough to rattle the chair. Navi set a steel case on the table, unfolding it slowly.

The receptionist sealed the door behind them, back braced, eyes watching corners. Knight stood at the head of the room, black hoodie, Timbs planted, presence heavier than the walls.

Simone crying. "Please! I can't, I didn't mean…"

Knight's voice dropped low, final. "You meant every move."

Navi peeled back the black cloth. She set the hot iron in the cradle, coils glowing red.

Simone's scream rose high, wild. "No, no! Please, I'll disappear, I'll never… "

Cam leaned close, her voice like a closing argument. "This isn't revenge. This is correction."

Jenx stepped forward, glove tight, hand wrapping the handle.

She didn't look angry; she looked certain.

Navi whispered, "Check."

Jenx lowered the iron, voice flat. "Mate."

A hiss cracked through the silence. Simone's scream shredded her throat.

Smoke curled up, and the Knight's mark burned deep into her forehead.

Jenx set the iron back in the cradle, steady as a ritual.

Banks checked her pulse.

Strong.

Alive.

Marked.

Knight's hood tilted. "She breathes. She remembers. She never touches Halo again."

The receptionist opened the door.

One by one, they walked out in all black hoodies.

Timbs heavy, moving like one clocked machine.

Simone sagged against the steel.

Tears streaking down her face.

The metallic stench of her own skin branded the room.

Brooklyn made its move.

BLACK SITE

Thursday | 12:12 a.m.

There were no clocks in the room.

Just concrete walls sealed behind a 3-inch-thick acrylic mirror that never fogged, even when she screamed.

A cot, bolted to the floor.

A metal sink-and-toilet combo.

No shower.

No hot water. No cold water.

Just lukewarm water on a slow drip.

The woman didn't cry anymore. That stopped around Day 12.

Now, she traced the mark on her forehead with trembling fingers, trying to remember what her own name used to taste like.

All she could taste was metal.

The knight symbol branded into her forehead burned slowly.

Her reflection didn't blink unless she did.

"You're not real," she whispered to it. "You're not real…"

The entire room seemed to shift, as if it had always been part of something larger,

like a set piece on a chessboard too vast to see.

The ceiling speaker crackled. Static.

A voice. Low. Male. Crisp Brooklyn lilt.

"Day 30. You're still alive. That's progress."

She sat up.

"Knight?" she rasped.

No reply.

Only footsteps now.

Not fast. Not loud.

Measured. Timed. Like strategy.

Then, silence.

A second voice, female, calm to the point of menace, filled the room.

"Let's begin your re-education."

Click.

A projector ignited. Shadows bled across the wall.

Photo after photo:

Monroe.

Cam.

Jinx.

Navi.

Knight.

Banks.

…And her.

Then …

A seventh file.

Confidential. Redacted. Unreadable.

Only one thing remained:

A single letter.

S.

Level 7 Access Only.

Her pulse spiked.

"Who the hell is that?"

Before she could blink, the room went black.

The floor beneath her feet glowed with the image of a knight chess piece, just like the one branded on her forehead.

KNIGHT

Knight & Monroe's Home | DUMBO, Brooklyn

Thursday | 2:27 a.m.

The night had been long.

Too long.

Knight slid the key into the front door, turning it slowly, the muscle in his jaw ticking.

The house was quiet. Too quiet.

Something wasn't right.

That's when he saw it.

The ring box unlocked and opened on top of a velvet-textured ivory envelope on the entry table.

No postage. No markings. Heavy.

He picked it up.

Cold in his hand.

Tore it open.

A single photograph and a positive pregnancy test.

Monroe.

Tied.

Gagged.

Eyes wide, but unbroken.

Beneath it, in 24k gold embossed letters pressed into the white velvet card stock.

When a Knight leaves the Queen vulnerable, it leads to loss.

Centered at the bottom, larger than the rest:

CHECKMATE!

www.ingramcontent.com/pod-product-compliance
Lightning Source LLC
Chambersburg PA
CBHW050358030726
47503CB00006B/1922